UNIVERSAL PICTURES PRESENTS

A GORDON COMPANY /

DAVIS ENTERTAIN

LICHT AND M

A KEVIN RE

KEVIN C

"WATERWORLD"

DENNIS HOPPER

JEANNE TRIPPLEHORN

TINA MAJORINO

MUSIC BY MARK ISHAM COSTUME DESIGNER JOHN BLOOMFIELD

LINE PRODUCER GENE LEVY FILM EDITOR PETER BOYLE

PRODUCTION DESIGNER DENNIS GASSNER

DIRECTOR OF PHOTOGRAPHY DEAN SEMLER A.C.S.

EXECUTIVE PRODUCERS JEFFREY MUELLER

ANDREW LICHT AND ILONA HERZBERG

WRITTEN BY PETER RADER AND DAVID TWOHY

PRODUCED BY CHARLES GORDON · JOHN DAVIS

KEVIN COSTNER

DIRECTED BY KEVIN REYNOLDS

A UNIVERSAL RELEASE

© 1995 UNIVERSAL CITY STUDIOS, INC.

DIGITAL dts SOUND

DTS STEREO
IN SELECTED THEATERS

Original Soundtrack on
MCA CDs & Cassettes

UNIVERSAL
AN MCA COMPANY

D0734189

**A Young Adult Novel
by Max Allan Collins**

**Based on the motion picture written by
Peter Rader and David Twohy**

BOULEVARD BOOKS, NEW YORK

FOR RACHEL LEMIEUX—
the best in any language

WATERWORLD

A Boulevard Book / published by arrangement with
MCA Publishing Rights, a division of MCA, Inc.

PRINTING HISTORY
Boulevard Young Adult edition / July 1995

ISBN: 1-57297-002-2

BOULEVARD
Boulevard Books are published by The Berkley Publishing Group,
200 Madison Avenue, New York, New York 10016.
Boulevard and the "B" design
are trademarks belonging to Berkley Publishing Group.

PRINTED IN THE UNITED STATES OF AMERICA

10 9 8 7 6 5 4 3

PROLOGUE

They say before the polar ice caps melted, people dwelled in "cities" on land. They lived and worked in towering structures called buildings, higher than a dozen windmills.

Families lived together in dwellings that would put our huts to shame. Ribbons of rock ran through the land oceans, connecting city and country. Land boats roamed these solid streams, with go-juice as plentiful as water. When was this? How long ago? It was before the world was thought to be covered with water.

That long.

But this tale, my children, is not of those ancient times. It is of the more recent past, a past I can remember. Hard it may be for you to imagine a time when my face was smooth and my brow unwrinkled. But even the eldest of Elders was once a child.

Once upon a time, when I was a child, I encountered the legendary figure you revere as "the Mariner."

He was not afraid of anything or anyone, and he could hear for a hundred miles—underwater. He could hide in the shadow of a noon sun—and he could be standing behind you and you wouldn't know it—not till it was too late. . . .

Don't be frightened. He was a hero. He was the bravest man in Waterworld, and he wasn't even a man at all. . . .

1

The gentle wind made for perfect trawling weather.

The Mariner was tempted to dive in for a pleasure swim. It was hot enough for that. But even as fast as he could swim—and no one was faster—he knew his ship could leave him behind in an instant.

The trimaran was a ragtag vessel with a single, eggbeater sail, gliding through the smoothness of an endless sapphire ocean. The ship was made of aluminum, plastic, and fiberglass—the fossils of an earlier time, patched together into a forty-foot craft as weathered as its captain. Its three hulls were connected with a netting that made up the ship's deck.

He lived here, on his nameless ship. His clay-potted lime plant was his only company. Wind chimes fashioned from ancient computer boards tinkled, and a harmonica mounted on the prow played a ghostly melody. Clothing, washed in the salt water, twisted on a line in the breeze.

The Mariner wore cutoff jeans, a knife in a sheath, and a shell earring. His features were hard and handsome, but his eyes were slits under a furrowed brow. His brown hair brushed his shoulders.

A sudden lurch of the ship sent him nimbly racing to the stern. He could see the dragline pulled tight. An ancient, rusty gauge said that his net had snagged something. . . .

The Mariner plucked a rubber salvage bag from the deck, and grabbed his tool belt. He took a few moments to gather deep breaths. Standing on feet with webbed toes, he flexed the gills behind his ears, beneath the flowing hair.

Then he dove over the side.

Ten minutes later, the salvage bag popped up on the surface, near the trimaran. Then the Mariner's head bobbed up, too.

He pulled himself up and onto the deck, dripping wet. He placed a few of the choicer treasures onto the deck—a bent ski pole, a broken ski, a pair of laced-together ski boots.

The rest of his bounty remained out there in the floating bag. It was brimming with treasure, including both glass and plastic bottles. He'd have to tug his bag up on deck, too, or before long it would drift out of reach.

He focused on one tiny, precious item; the Mariner

had heard other traders call these little round sticks "lighters."

He flicked it. A flame jumped from the object's tip, and he smiled.

His boat creaked.

He flew to the harpoon gun, mounted on the bow, and swung it toward the sound.

He saw a patched-together ship, smaller than his, that must have glided up while he was below. Alone on the ship was a drifter in scraps of leather and cloth. Had he taken advantage of the Mariner's absence for some looting?

The drifter was frozen in the sights of the harpoon gun.

"I didn't board you," the drifter said. "I wouldn't do such a thing."

The Mariner kept the gun trained on the drifter, but risked a glance around the trimaran. Nothing seemed missing.

"You were down there a long time," the drifter said. "Thought maybe something happened to you . . ."

"Or were you hoping?"

"No, friend, I wish bad luck on no man . . . except maybe Smokers."

Smokers were the worst breed of pirate in Waterworld, barbarians ruled by a vicious madman called the Deacon.

The Mariner's salvage bag was floating past the drifter's ship. Did the drifter notice it?

"Your boat looks familiar," the Mariner said. "I've seen it before—but not you."

"Its previous owner didn't need it no more."

"Why is that?"

"He was dead, friend. I took it legal—salvage rights." The drifter shrugged. "Just improvin' my means. Can't blame a man."

"At least in my case, you waited. I owe you that much."

Raggedy half-gloved hands patted the air. "No, no . . . you owe me nothin', friend. I got all the supplies I need. See, I just come from an atoll . . . eight days due east."

The Mariner nodded, and looked toward the eastern horizon as his salvage bag drifted away. "Two of our kind meet, something's got to be exchanged."

"I know the code as well as you, friend. But I'll give you this one for free."

There was something out there, on the horizon. "Nothing's free in Waterworld," the Mariner said.

Two puffs of smoke curled from distant dots on the water. But across that water came a sound that seemed much closer: engines.

The drifter heard it, too.

"Smokers . . ." the drifter whispered, eyes wide with fear.

"Luck to you," the Mariner said.

"And to you!" the drifter said, adjusting his sail. And, with that, the raggedy ship was moving off.

The Mariner was looking at his floating salvage bag.

"It's not worth it, friend!" the drifter called, shaking his head. Two small green objects tumbled out of his shirt.

The Mariner flashed a look at his lime tree and saw it had been stripped of its fruit.

But the drifter's ship was well on its way now.

"See, you paid me after all, friend!" he called.

The Mariner turned to his steering console. He threw levers. The eggbeater sail folded into the mast, which extended to twice its height. Sails unfurled as the trawler magically transformed itself into a sleek racing yacht.

Heading straight for the bobbing booty bag, the trimaran cut across the glassy surface like a speeding arrow.

Others were bearing down on the booty bag, too.

Those dots on the horizon had blossomed into a horrible quartet. The four barely dressed brutes were Smokers. Fierce as they were stupid, they rode go-juice-burning water jetskis whose smoking engines tore the placid afternoon to shreds.

The trimaran was flying at forty knots when the ship rounded the salvage bag. A long pole in hand, the

7

Mariner snagged the bag, even as the ship was coming about hard.

Then the trimaran was going in the opposite direction.

And the four pirates on jetskis almost tumbled off their perches as they brought their little crafts around to take pursuit.

Up ahead he could see the drifter's ship. The Mariner charted a collision course.

The drifter heard the engines approaching and tried desperately to pick up some speed.

But the Mariner's trimaran was closing on him.

And the Smokers were ripping across the water, zeroing in on the Mariner.

The drifter yelped as the trimaran suddenly drenched him and his ship. The trimaran's nearest outrigger hull lifted over the ship like the wing of a bird, snapping the smaller boat's mainmast.

Looking back at the crestfallen captain of the now-floundering ship, the Mariner raised a scolding finger and sent the man a stern look.

You don't break the code.

The Smokers had, as the Mariner knew they would, abandoned their pursuit of him in favor of swooping in on this easier, wounded prey.

"He shouldn't have taken the limes," the Mariner said to himself.

After all, nothing was free in Waterworld.

2

A week and a day later, the trimaran approached a walled, circular, floating city. Golden in the glow of a glorious afternoon sun, this trash heap of a town rose from the hulls of derelict boats. Constructed from scraps of metal, wood, plastic and canvas, settlements like these were called "atolls" in Waterworld.

The trimaran was in trawler mode, its eggbeater sail slowly turning. As his ship glided into the area before towering twin gates, the Mariner hoisted a green flag that identified him as a trader.

The Mariner had made himself presentable. He looked prosperous in his armless leather-and-canvas jacket, fish-skin pants and ski-boots.

His goods were laid out for inspection on the deck: hubcaps, a yo-yo, a broken clarinet, antique silver discs called CDs, and more ancient trash that had become modern treasure.

Slinging a leather pouch on a strap, he looked up

9

hopefully at a bearded gatesman on the parapet above. Near the gatesman stood a broad-shouldered, burned-brown figure. This was the atoll's Enforcer. Every atoll had such a guardian at the gate.

"Afraid the flag's down, drifter," the Enforcer called down. "We got enough traders in Oasis."

So that was the atoll's name: Oasis.

The Mariner pulled up the leather pouch. Then he removed the lid from the heavy jar, scooping up the priceless substance therein.

The aroma drifted up and tickled the nostrils of the bearded gatesman and the burly Enforcer. They could not stop their smiles.

"Dirt," the gatesman sighed.

The Mariner smiled, too—just a little.

"Open the gates for him," the Enforcer said.

Nothing on Waterworld—not even the tastiest grilled fish—could compare to the scent of dirt.

Soon the tall iron gates swung open for the trimaran, and the ship eased into the atoll's lagoon.

The blades of a windmill churned the air lazily, casting their reflection on the lagoon's surface. The windmill was the source of electricity in this floating village, and was its highest structure.

The trimaran's easy glide and sleek design caught the eyes of the Atollers. They were solemn, sullen people, their patchwork clothing running to dreary grays and browns. There were no greetings from these water city denizens. Merely stares—some curious, others openly distrustful.

Before long, the trimaran slipped alongside a sprawling "organo" barge; such barges were a bad-smelling fixture in any atoll. An organo barge was part compost heap, part fruit garden, and part cemetery.

Under a massive, mournful tree, grieving citizens and a few church Elders were attending the funeral service of an elderly woman.

"Too old for life she was," an Elder said, "this woman does now leave us. . . ."

The old woman's body began to sink into the compost heap. The mourners used garden hoes to begin tending rows of fruits and vegetables around her.

The Mariner guided his craft toward a dock. These Atollers were a superstitious lot, the Mariner knew. Living day to day, clinging to survival, they needed something to believe in.

The Mariner preferred to believe in himself.

He was securing his ship when a menacing shadow fell across him. The Mariner looked up at a man who seemed taller than that windmill.

"Remember me?" the Enforcer asked casually.

The Mariner stood. "I know who you are. What you are."

"Good. You have two hours here in Oasis."

"I only need one."

11

"Less is your choice. More is an infraction. Understood?"

The Mariner nodded.

The trading barge was nearby. As the Mariner made his way there, a Pied Piper's trail of Atollers followed behind him. Word of his jar of precious dirt had spread across the village like fire chasing oil.

The trading post was part tavern, part store. One counter served as a bar for dispensing various grades of water—or "hydro," as it was called in Waterworld. Another, off to one side, served as a sort of bank.

The dirt from the jar was poured out on a scale. It was weighed precisely, and handled with a delicacy deserving of so precious a commodity.

"Seven point nine kilos," the banker whispered. His eyes were wide with greed and amazement. "Pure."

A gasp came from the crowd of Atollers. Long ago, gold and silver had been considered precious. In Waterworld, gold and silver had no practical use. Both would sink like the stones they were.

But dirt was something wonderful . . .

"How'd you come by so much of it?" the banker asked.

The Mariner shrugged. "Another atoll."

"Hmmm," the banker said. "Where'd *they* get it?"

"Didn't say."

From the crowd, a scrawny male Atoller called, "I

heard about that place! Smokers raided 'em! They was all *killed!*"

"That's why they didn't say," the Mariner said.

Worried murmuring passed across the crowd like a wave.

The Mariner pointed at the pile of dirt balancing on the scale. "Are we talking or trading?"

"How about we figure it like it was pure hydro?" the banker offered. "Sixty-two chits—that goes a long way, here in Oasis."

"Twice that goes further," the Mariner said. "And that's what I want."

And that's what he got.

At the rear of the trading post, the tavern was tended by a slender, beautiful woman called Helen. Her large clear eyes were as dark as her lovely hair, which was braided back. Around her neck was a beaded necklace, and her dress was made of netting.

Many people in Oasis had long ago lost all hope, but not Helen. She was driven by her belief in the ancient myth of a place called Dryland.

That belief—and a very special orphaned child she had been raising—gave her the courage to believe in a better tomorrow.

Right now she was serving hydro to a pair of scruffy traders leaning against the bar.

"What's so great about dirt?" the younger of the two asked the other. "You can't eat it."

13

Helen poured them both a murky tumblerful of grade-three hydro. "You can eat the fruit or vegetables that grow from it," she offered.

"True enough," the younger trader said. "But the amounts you can find won't grow you much of anything. See?" He gestured to a scrawny tomato plant in a pot on one of the nearly bare shelves behind the bar.

"It isn't what you can *do* with the dirt," Helen said. "It's what it stands for . . . and the *promise* it holds."

"Promise?" the younger trader asked.

"Yes," she said, "and the question the dirt asks . . . '*where did I come from?*'"

"Dryland," the older trader said reverently.

"A jug," a harsh voice said.

Helen looked up into the hard, cold blue eyes of a muscular trader in sharkskin garb. His features were handsome but cruel, his hair shoulder-length blond. Under the tan, the man's flesh was fair. He was a Nord.

"Grade two," the Nord said.

"It'll cost you three chits," she said.

He dug out the coins and grabbed the water jug from her. Then he went over to a table where a pitiful, balding wreck of a man was waiting.

What was a thriving trader doing, consorting with a tattered beggar like that? she wondered.

The Nord sat next to the raggedy old man, and poured a murky tumbler of hydro.

14

But when the old man reached for the glass, the Nord gripped the beggar's bony wrist—hard.

"First," the Nord said, "you tell me."

"It's the child," the old man whispered.

"What child?"

"That woman." The old man pointed.

The Nord looked toward Helen, who was serving another round to the two traders.

"Are we talking about a woman," the Nord said impatiently, "or a child?"

"The woman is raisin' a child. The child ain't hers, she's from somewheres else."

"Another atoll, you mean?"

"No. That's just it . . ." Now the old man's eyes opened. Though they were as murky as the hydro in the glass before him, those eyes glittered. "Dryland."

The Nord snorted. "Dryland's a fairy tale."

"Maybe. But this child, she's got marks . . . tattoos, inkings . . . on her back. They say, if you know how to read 'em, it's like a *map* . . ."

"You talk dryrot, old man . . ."

But the old man was staring at him intensely. "There are some around who still believe. I heard some traders say that . . . *certain* people got an eye out for the child."

"What 'certain people'?"

"You know. Smokers."

The Nord smiled at him. "We wouldn't want to cross

15

them, would we? Best keep all of this to ourselves, old man."

And he pushed the glass of hydro toward the old man.

"You are a generous and kind man, sir!"

The old man began greedily gulping down the fluid, even as another trader was walking up to the bar.

The Mariner.

As the Mariner stepped to the counter, Helen was careful to hide her interest in this stranger who'd brought that precious dirt to Oasis.

"Help you?" she asked.

"Maybe you could direct me to the store."

She knew how pitifully bare the shelves behind her were.

"Afraid you're lookin' at it," she said.

"I'll take all the hydro you've got in storage."

She frowned. "You'll close me down . . ."

"You'd run out sooner or later, wouldn't you? Got any canvas? Any line?"

"We got line," she said, "but it's hair. No canvas."

"Any bread?"

"No."

"Wood?"

"Just the shelves on the wall, stranger."

The stranger slumped, disappointed that his chits could buy so little here in Oasis.

"How about that drink?" she asked, almost feeling

sorry for him. "I still got a few bottles you didn't buy."

"Make it a tall one. The good stuff." He threw a chit on the counter.

She was pouring him a tumbler of clear water when that Nord trader suddenly sidled up to the bar.

The Nord touched her wrist. "Make it two. A man this rich'll buy a glass for a fellow traveler, I'm sure."

She pulled her wrist away and frowned at the Nord.

The Mariner said, quietly, "Just one."

The Nord stared at the Mariner with a smile. But Helen didn't believe the smile—she had a feeling that the Mariner's slight would not be soon forgotten by the Nord.

She refilled the glass.

"So, Dirt Man," the Nord said, "how long you been out?"

The Mariner looked coldly at the Nord and said nothing.

"Talk is free," the Nord said.

"Nothing's free in Waterworld," the Mariner said.

"I'm just making friendly conversation. How long you been out?"

"Fifteen lunars."

"Fifteen lunars? Are you kidding?"

The Mariner turned to look at him, slowly. "Does it look like I 'kid'?"

A child came out from behind the tarp of the storeroom in back of the counter. She couldn't have been older than seven. Her skin was darker than that of the lady bartender, though her netting apparel was similar.

The girl moved to a stove and swung it open. She dug inside, fishing out bits of charcoal.

As the girl bent over the stove, the back of her tunic slipped down, revealing something. *What was it?* the Mariner wondered. *A birth mark?*

No, the Mariner thought, *those are tattoos*. A dark circle, a jagged peak, an arrow, with letters that looked oriental . . .

The Mariner was not the only one who noticed this. The Nord's eyes were wide, and he had moved so close to the counter, he was almost climbing over it.

"Enola!" Helen called to the girl.

"I need another drawstick," the child said.

Helen knelt and guided the girl to her feet. She pulled the girl's tunic up, covering the markings.

"I'll bring you one," Helen said, steering her to the back room. "You just stay in back, now . . . only grown-ups out here."

"So," the Nord said to the Mariner, conversationally, "as I was saying—"

"Why are you talking to me?"

The Nord's grin had nothing to do with smiling. "Just being friendly."

"I don't have friends," the Mariner said.

18

The Nord thought about that. Then he shrugged and wandered away from the counter.

"You ready for another drink?" Helen asked the Mariner.

"This'll hold me." He looked past her. "That tomato plant . . . How much?"

She thought for a moment, then said, "Half your chits."

He nodded without hesitation.

She was plucking the plant off the shelf when he added, "I'll take them, too."

"Take what? You bought everything but the shelves!"

"That's what I mean," he said. "I'll take them, too."

19

3

The shelves in a net bag slung over his one shoulder, the Mariner stepped from the trading post into the afternoon sunshine. The potted tomato plant was under his arm. Around him was the milling life, the people, of the community that was Oasis. Fisherwomen repaired their nets, men patched a hole in the wharf. Kids ran and played, their voices echoing off the water.

But this wasn't for him. He was an outsider here; he headed for home—his trimaran.

Rapid footsteps clomping on the wharf behind him made him whirl. Was it the Nord, looking for trouble?

Helen was startled by how quickly he turned to her.

"Something wrong?" he asked her. "I paid you in full, didn't I?"

"Yes . . . of course. I just . . . wanted to talk to you, away from the others."

"Why?"

"You said you were out there—" She pointed across

the golden lagoon, toward the gates. "—fifteen lunars."

"Yes. So?"

"What have you seen out there, in your fifteen lunars?"

"What might I have seen, besides fish and ocean and an occasional boat?"

"An end," she said, her voice a hopeful whisper. "An end to all this water . . ."

"You're asking the wrong person."

"What do you mean?"

Now he pointed across the lagoon, where the organo barge floated. "Ask the old woman they buried," he said. "She found the only true end."

Her face fell. "I don't believe that."

"Good for you," he said, and moved on. He listened for her footsteps, but she wasn't following him.

As he rounded the dock with his trimaran in clear sight, he saw a reception committee of half a dozen Elders. .

The Elders were staring at him with fear and suspicion, and a crowd of Atollers was gathering on the wharf nearby.

A gaunt Elder stepped forward to begin questioning him. But the Mariner had no interest in the fears or concerns of these people, and he walked right by them.

The trimaran was just ahead as a hard hand grabbed

his shoulder from behind. He flicked the hand off, and turned. He found himself facing one of the gatesmen.

"When the Elders give the word, you can leave. Not before."

The Mariner swung the netted bag of shelves into the gatesman, knocking him down, and moved quickly on. But then powerful arms locked him from behind, causing the net bag of shelving to clatter to the dock. His precious tomato plant tumbled there as well.

Suddenly a trio of male Atollers group-tackled him, dragging him to the dock. The Mariner twisted his neck, fighting a choking grip and working his mouth around to where he could take a big, deep bite.

The guy screamed and released the choke hold, but grabbed with both hands at the Mariner's long hair, and yanked up. The hair fell away from the Mariner's neck, revealing the secret there.

The gill behind the Mariner's ear.

"Shades below!" the Atoller said. "He's a *mute-o*!"

And the Mariner looked up into three horrified faces.

And he could hear an alarm being raised as the High Elder shouted, "*Mutation!*"

If he didn't get away *right now,* he was dead.

He lashed out at the nearest face, and began throwing kicks and punches. Then he was on his feet, with dozens of hands and arms clinging to him. But he squirmed and thrashed his way free.

He'd have to forget the trimaran, for now at least. He

needed to get underwater, where he could breathe and they could not.

"*Don't let him get to the water!*" the High Elder cried.

Blocking his way were a gang of Atollers ready to bring him down in another tackle. They were getting ready to spring.

So he sprang first.

He leaped right over them, clearing them by inches. Then he splashed into the deep, clear, cold lagoon. He could swim under that gate and survive out there, until some trader gave him a lift . . .

Then, above him, all around, were splashes and spurts of foam as Atollers dove in, surrounding him. And a net large enough to snag the trimaran itself came cascading down. He whirled, hoping to dive deeper than the net or the Atollers could follow.

But it was too late.

The net was around him, and they were yanking it tight.

Like a fly in a spider's web, he was caught, squirming. He used his knife to try to cut the netting, but got nowhere.

Soon, men on the dock above were hooking the net—and him—with their gaffs, pulling him in. They tugged him up on the dock, just another flopping fish. Their big catch.

Through the netting he could see them—not just a crowd now, but a mob, of angry faces, frightened faces.

Only one sympathetic face could he find: the woman. Helen.

The net came off as a rope looped him around the neck, around the gills, and yanked tight.

Then, just as he thought he would be choked to death, a blade sliced through the rope. The Mariner fell to his knees, gasping for air.

Above him, glaring at the crowd, was the Enforcer, a huge blade in his fist.

"By what right—" the High Elder began, stepping up to the Enforcer.

"You pay me to keep the peace, don't you?"

"He is a mutation. He needs to be destroyed."

"That may be," the Enforcer said. "But not here and not like this."

The Mariner watched as the High Elder thought that over.

"If you're not going to follow your own laws," the Enforcer said, "I'll seek out another atoll. I'm sure my services will—"

"That won't be necessary," the High Elder said quickly. Good enforcers were hard to find.

"Cage him," the High Elder said.

Then they hauled the Mariner away, with the mob following along.

In the moonlight, the organo barge had a silvery beauty. The gnarled tree extended its many arms over

25

the barge's paltry gardens like a ghost unsure whether to haunt or protect.

The Mariner was suspended over the pier in an iron cage. The cage was large enough for him to stand in and small enough that he could not lie down comfortably. He had tested the bars—and the padlock—and saw no means of escape. Swaying in a cool evening breeze, he hung there, helpless.

The post that suspended him extended up through a platform. An open stairway gave the townspeople access to a walkway near the cage. They could gawk at their prisoner, or curse at him, or pelt him with things.

And some of them had.

But, from time to time, in the window of the windmill tower, he saw a sympathetic face. It was the child—that dark, pretty, mysterious child from the tavern.

What had that woman Helen called the girl?

Enola.

A loud creaking startled him, but it was only gears within the windmill. Soon coils within jars atop poles along the wharf walkway came alive. The street-lamps cast a yellowish glow, giving the atoll a strange beauty.

With this added light, he could make out his trimaran much better. His ship. His home . . .

There were people on his deck! They'd boarded under the cover of night, and were exposed by the streetlamps.

He stood, clutching the bars of his tiny prison, and it swayed. His mouth opened to yell an objection, but what good would it have done?

Helpless, he watched as atollers hopped off the trimaran with armloads of his possessions, scurrying away like rats into the night.

"Hard luck, Dirt Man," someone said.

The Mariner's eyes traveled to the lagoon nearby. A little boat was being rowed past him by the grinning Nord. The boat eased its way to the main gates, which groaned open, then rumbled shut.

Muffled voices reached him from a covered boat off to his left. Earlier, he had seen both atollers and the Elders gradually entering the Atoll Meeting Hall. Helen had been among them.

Perhaps his fate was being decided within, even now.

Within the meeting hall, the High Elder, Priam, sat with his brethren at a main table. Atollers crowded around, milling with the excitement of trapping and catching a mutation.

"The evidence speaks for itself," Priam said. "We must dispense with the mute-o as soon as possible."

There were nods and murmurs of agreement, but one voice rang out above them: "But he brought *dirt*!"

"We have seen dirt before," Priam said, "from other traders—"

"Not *pure* like this," Helen said. "What if it came from Dryland?"

"He came from the west," the bearded gatesman said.

"The west!" a male Atoller shouted. "That's where the Smokers come from!"

"Then perhaps the mute-o is a Smoker spy," Priam said.

All eyes turned to him.

"You have no evidence of that," Helen said.

She turned to address the crowd.

"Our gardens are dying," she said, "our machines are breaking down. This place—this whole way of living—is coming to an end. Now we have someone in our midst who might be able to show us the way to a new place, a new *land*—"

"Dryland is a hoax!" the High Elder lashed out. "A myth, a children's fairy tale! And it is long since past time, Helen, that you accept that fact. The sooner you do, the better off we'll all be!"

The bearded gatesman stepped forward. "We'd be better off if we got rid of that *child* of hers, too!"

The murmuring was back again, uglier now.

"Those marks on the child's back," the gatesman said, "they attract talk—they attract trouble! They say the Smokers are looking for her!"

Fear clutched Helen's chest. She gave up all hope of

28

reasoning with this mob, and rushed from the meeting hall.

Perhaps Old Gregor would know what to do. . . .

In a loft workshop within the windmill tower, a white-bearded, slightly stooped old man gazed through a big, homemade telescope. It was aimed, as any good telescope should be, into the heavens. Around him in the workshop were tables cluttered with bottles and tubes and flasks.

Gregor was his name, and he had been granted this generous space by the Elders because he was the designer of the windmill whose gears powered the atoll's electricity.

Enola was forty feet below him, sitting at a table by a window. She was caught up in her favorite pastime: drawing.

Using a piece of charcoal—a "drawstick"—she drew directly on the table. Gregor recognized a good number of the images she created. He'd seen them in ancient magazines, and knew that these were glimpses of life on land: *plants and waterfalls and birds and beasts* . . .

Could these all flow just from the child's imagination?

As he moved down the winding wooden walkway, he wondered if the things she saw were visions. And if so, were they visions of the past, of the future . . . or perhaps even of a present, just beyond the horizon?

Gregor felt sure the charcoal sketches reported things this girl had seen. Just as right now she was drawing a man in a hanging cage.

Gregor stroked the child's hair. She looked back up at him with wide eyes of a deep, dark blue that only the ocean at its most dangerous depths could rival.

"I don't mean to bother you, child," he said, lifting her long hair. He needed to have another look at the markings, just below her neck.

He stared at the tattoo. Was it a map? A calendar? Or something his insufficient intellect hadn't even yet thought of?

A side door opened and he knew it was Helen.

"Back so soon?" Gregor asked.

Helen crossed the room, skirting the metal throne that was part of Gregor's latest—and most important—project.

She whispered to him, "We've got to get out of here."

He took her gently by the arm and walked her away from the doodling child. "I take it the meeting did not go well."

"They're putting us adrift, Gregor."

"They wouldn't dare cast me out," Gregor huffed. "I'd shut down their power so fast—"

"Not you." She whispered again. "Enola and me."

"They won't hurt you," he assured her. "They know I'd turn their lights off if they did!"

She cast her eyes toward the odd metal throne. "How long till we leave?"

He looked upward, thought about it, calculated . . .

"Another week," he said. "Ideally."

"We don't have a week," she said. "We'll be lucky to have tonight!"

"But, Helen . . . I don't know where to *go* yet!"

They looked toward Enola, as the child sat drawing with her piece of charcoal.

"I know the child bears the answer we seek," Gregor said, "if I could just solve the puzzle on her back." He shook his head. "I just don't know *how* . . ."

"Maybe," Enola said, "*he* does."

The girl was leaning forward, looking out the window, pointing to the man hanging in the iron cage in the moonlight.

Gregor, lantern in hand, went up the stairs of the platform to the half-circle walkway. He paused at the railing, near the dangling cage and its silent, seated occupant.

The old man fished a magnifying glass from his loose clothing. Then he leaned against the rail to get a closer look at the feet of the mutated man.

"Ah yes," Gregor said, not to the Mariner, but to himself. "They *are* webbed, aren't they? You're the genuine article, all right! Ichthyus Sapien! *You* can breathe in *water*."

But the Mariner said nothing.

"Don't like humans much, do you?" Gregor sighed. "Can't say I blame you. But are *all* your kind so unfriendly?"

"I have no kind," the Mariner said.

"Oh, fishrot," Gregor said. "I'd be shocked if there weren't others."

That caught the Mariner's attention. Had he never found others of his kind, Gregor wondered?

"If there *aren't* any of your kind right now, my boy," Gregor said, "there will be eventually. Give nature a little time to catch up with you."

The Mariner turned away.

"About that dirt of yours," Gregor said. "Where'd it come from? Not . . . Dryland, by any chance?"

But the Mariner didn't reply.

From a pocket, Gregor took a piece of paper. On it was a charcoal sketch of the tattoo on Enola's back.

"Do you know what it means?" Gregor asked. "Can you read it?"

After a long pause, the Mariner asked, "If I tell you, will you open this padlock?"

Gregor frowned. "If I do let you out, can I trust you?"

"I won't hurt anyone," he said. "I'll just answer your questions . . . and leave."

Just then a voice boomed out: "*Gregor!*"

The old man was immediately caught in a beam of light.

Shouting from a watchtower, shining a spotlight on the old man, was the atoll Enforcer.

"*What's your business there?*"

"Nothing! Just having a look at your captive!"

"*Well, get inside! It'll soon be curfew.*"

"I'm sorry," the old man whispered to the Mariner. "I'm not a brave man . . . If you know anything about Dryland, I beg of you, tell me now!"

The Mariner turned his back on the inventor, settled himself in his cage and closed his eyes.

Gregor stood there for several long moments, searching for the words that might stir this creature.

Then the watch bell clanged across the water, echoing through the atoll, announcing curfew.

And, defeated, the old man dragged himself home.

4

The sound of footsteps wakened Helen. She patted the bedside beside her.

The girl was gone.

Fear clutched her chest and she sprang from the bed, the threatening words of the Elders and Atollers echoing in her brain.

"Enola!" she called. "Eno—"

But there the child was, at a window. The walls around her, in their living quarters here in the trading barge, were littered with charcoal images that had leaped from the child's imagination. Or her memory . . .

Helen went to the window and touched the girl lightly on the shoulder.

"What will they do to him?" Enola asked.

The both could see the procession of Elders, slowly marching, and the Atollers falling in behind them. They were approaching the platform where the Mariner stood clutching the bars of his dangling cage.

Enola said, "They're going to bury him, aren't they?"

"Don't watch."

"Not watching won't make it not happen," Enola said. "We should help him."

The Mariner stood facing the Elders gathered along the half-circle walkway of the platform.

"After considerable deliberation of the evidence," Priam said, "we have come to our decision—"

"Nice of you to let me know how my trial came out," the Mariner said. "Sorry I couldn't be there."

Priam raised his head, ignoring the prisoner. "In the best interest of public safety, and the greater good, this 'mute-o' is hereby sentenced to be recycled."

There were murmurs of assent from the crowd.

"Proceed," Priam said, "in the customary fashion . . ."

The Mariner heard the grinding of gears and felt his one-cell prison shifting, swaying. Above him, a boom was swinging him out, carrying him over the organo barge.

"Bones to berries, veins to vines," Priam intoned.

Lowering him, now.

The ooze was coming up through the iron bars of the cage's floor. He began climbing the sides of the cage, but there just wasn't room to go anywhere.

"Recycled and entombed . . ." Priam went on.

36

At least he was sinking slowly. The stuff was as thick as it was foul, and this would take a while.

Though suffocating shouldn't take long at all.

In a watchtower, through a viewing scope, a watchman did what watchmen do: kept watch.

In Oasis, there could be no more boring job than studying that endless, unchanging sea. For days on end, your eyes could search the water and see only . . . sea.

But right now something had turned up, not visible at first, because it was in line with the sun.

Smoke curled skyward, seeming to rise from the water.

"*Smokers!*" the watchman screamed.

The slime was up to his ankles now, and the Mariner didn't make out the word the watchman screamed.

Everyone else in Oasis did.

Everyone—including the normally dignified Elders— scattered in every direction, like pieces of a shattered glass.

The Mariner was a problem instantly forgotten.

But that didn't stop his cage from sinking further into the sludge.

Out on the ocean, closing in on the floating city, was a fleet of Smokers. They flew across the surface of the sea as if the water were a mere inconvenience to determined men with motors.

A beat-up seaplane led the way for speedboats and jetskis. Their engines ripped through the serenity of the sea with a loud rumbling roar.

Within the floating city, the denizens were running to their battle stations. Water cannons were manned, storm shutters were dropped, fire buckets doled out.

In the armory, men, women, and children pulled weapons from shelves and racks: bows and arrows, blades, spearguns, lances. There were no firearms, though all knew they'd be facing the firesticks of these fiercest of foes.

A horrified cry from a watchtower cut above the din of the approaching diesel-burners. *"Berserkers!"*

A chill coursed through Helen as she found a spear gun in the armory. She followed after Enola, who was scurrying up a walkway with her bow and arrows.

Berserkers, Helen thought. The horrible stories about these semihuman Smokers had seemed like tall tales . . .

Yet there they were, out on the sun-whitened water, huge brutes on water skis who shot off moving ramps to hurl themselves into the air. Then they would soar blindly over the walls of the atoll.

It seemed unreal, as she ducked down, a human-like creature rocketing over her head. Some Berserkers overshot fatally into a wall or roof. But others landed safely, splashing into the lagoon itself.

The cage had stopped sinking. All around the Mariner, battle reigned, and he could neither protect himself nor anyone else. He was a stationary target here . . .

A Smoker stood before him, pointing a handgun at him.

Well, the Mariner thought, *I don't have far to go to get to the graveyard . . .*

Then the Berserker shuddered, and fell to the walkway, a spear in his back.

Just behind him was the atoll Enforcer.

The Enforcer looked at the Mariner, who yelled, "Let me out of here! I can fight!"

But the Enforcer moved on.

Just then a Berserker on skis, flying over the wall, crash-landed on the Mariner's cage. The impact rendered the Berserker unconscious, and it did something else as well . . .

As it knocked into the cage, the added weight of the Berserker pushed it deeper into the organo pit . . . *And now the cage was sinking again!*

The Mariner reached a hand through the bars, up and around, and tugged a knife off the belt of the Berserker.

As the slime rose around him, he worked the blade in the padlock. The blade was under the surface of the ooze, but if he could only . . .

And then the blade snapped.

39

Helen and the child remained at their battle station. The atollers were fighting back effectively. Water cannons knocked jetskiers off their seats. Live jellyfish were dropped onto Smokers scaling the walls. Down below, bucket brigades were putting out spot fires.

"Helen!" Gregor's voice called across the noise of engines and gunfire. "*Helen!*"

The old man was waving to her from the workshop window.

"It's time!" he called. "It's time!"

She yanked Enola by the hand, and then they ran for the windmill.

That was when the top of the windmill exploded under a hailstorm of gunfire, raining down fiery fragments.

And the roof was gone, as if it had never been.

Hope and fear fought for control, as Helen clutched Enola's hand and wove along the wharf walkway through the hand-to-hand combat. At least the windmill had not caught fire, though smoke curled from the ragged opening where the rooftop had been.

Could Gregor even still be alive?

Had they been mere moments earlier, they would have found Gregor in the workshop. Sun streaming down on him, he had assembled the steering mechanism and affixed the propeller onto the crude engine behind the thronelike chair. Two side seats were attached for Helen and Enola.

But when Helen and Enola entered the windmill workshop, the putt-putting sound of the engine said they were too late.

Gregor was leaving without them.

He was above them, sitting behind the quilt-work bag filled with hot air. The contraption, a small "dirigible,"—a steerable balloon—was already six feet off the ground.

"Gregor—wait!"

"I waited as long as I could!" the old man cried. He had a hand on the steering device, but reached the other down to them. "A blast unmoored me!"

"Gregor!" Helen screamed. "No!"

"You can still make it!" the old man called.

But he was already too far above them.

"Please don't go away!" Enola called.

Helen jumped, tried to reach his hand. So did Enola. Helen's hand scraped Gregor's clutching fingers. . . .

They ran up the circling walkway, trying to catch him.

No use. No use.

"Forgive me!" he cried. "Forgive me . . ."

Then they were looking up, and the despondent Gregor was looking down, as the dirigible floated away, through the smashed roof and into the sky.

The Smoker gunner on the boat that had blown the roof off the windmill now took perfect aim at the escaping balloon.

But a jetski got in the way, and the explosion that followed created a smoke cloud so large, the dirigible disappeared behind it.

By the time the cloud had cleared, the balloon was out of range, and on its way to being a dot in the distant sky.

And the wreckage of the jetski hit the organo barge like a meteor, setting its tree on fire.

In the windmill tower, Helen grabbed Enola's hand. "We're not through yet," the woman said defiantly.

And they ran from the windmill.

Foul-smelling, sticky muck was oozing in all around the Mariner. But he didn't give up. He kept his face pushed up to the top of the cage, where there was still air.

And he saw a lovely face.

Helen had laid a hunk of plastic board across the organo pit. She was crouched there before him.

"If I get you out of here," she said, "will you take us with you?"

"If I get the boat," he said, "can you get the gate open?"

She nodded.

Then she took something from alongside her: a crowbar.

It was in his hands just as the muck swallowed him, and his cage, entirely.

Helen gasped, but Enola said, "Look!"

And a gooey-brown arm emerged, along one solid edge of the organo pit. A slimy hand took hold. The mariner, covered in brown-gray gunk, pulled himself up.

His eyes took in the raging battle. The atoll gates were shrouded in water-cannon mist. Several Smokers scurried about the deck of his trimaran for plunder, not knowing the Atollers had earlier beaten them to it.

"The gates," he reminded Helen. "They'll both have to be open, or my ship won't make it through. Understand?"

"I understand," Helen said.

Then he dove off the barge, into the lagoon.

Helen held Enola's hand as they moved along walkways toward the gate. Smokers were storming through a breach in one atoll wall. The Atollers were tragically outnumbered.

A cruelly handsome figure in sharkhide, blond hair so long it brushed his shoulders, strode down a walkway. He was leading a swarm of Smokers toward the trading-post barge.

The Nord, Helen thought. So *he* had been the Smoker spy.

43

The Elders had consigned the wrong stranger to the organo cemetery. But they had had little time to regret it. Even now, on the far walls, Smokers were slaying them.

The Mariner swam deep, cutting a sleek path toward the trimaran. Above him, bullets pinged the water, Smokers on jetskis streaked by. Underwater, these sounds seemed distant and unreal.

Bursting from the water like a leaping dolphin, the Mariner landed on the stern of his ship, almost at the feet of a looting Smoker.

Quicker than the blink of an eye, the Mariner knocked him cold and shoved him overboard.

Then, at his steering console, the Mariner threw levers, starting the eggbeater sail turning. Soon the trimaran was on a course with those massive, closed gates.

Where was that woman?

Then he saw her, nearing one of the twin gate towers, the child trailing along.

He hit levers and gears, and the trimaran began its transformation.

From the walkway high above, Helen felt a small hand grip her arm.

"Look!" Enola said.

The stranger's trawler had turned itself into a sleek sailboat!

"Wow," Enola said.

Looking past the transforming trimaran, Helen could see Atollers diving into the lagoon's waters. Some were in canoes, others in barrels, some swimming along in life buoys.

They needed the gates opened, too.

It was up to her, if any of them were to survive.

She bent to Enola. "When I throw that lever, and the gate begins to open, we have to run . . ."

She pointed to the narrow catwalk attached to the back of the gates. Right now, the walkway was one continuous bridge. But when one gate parted, the walkway would split in two.

Helen finished, ". . . and we'll have to jump. Understand?"

The child nodded.

"Try not to be afraid," Helen said, and squeezed the child's shoulder.

Enola said, "You, too."

Helen took a deep breath, then went inside the gate tower, and shoved the lever. Gears ground their teeth as the first gate began to rumble its way open.

"Let's go!" she yelled, grabbing the girl's hand, and began leading her down the narrow, moving catwalk.

The gate slowly began to open, but the Mariner knew he could not make it through until the other side swung open as well. Watching the woman and child scurry across the moving walkway, he guided his ship, keeping down. Bullets pinged the water and clanged off metal on the trimaran.

Just then a Smoker's riderless jetski crashed right into the unopened section of gate.

"Hurry!" he called up to the woman and child.

They had paused at the edge of the catwalk where it ended.

"Jump!" he yelled.

They jumped. As they did, gunfire stitched its way across the wreckage of the crashed jetski. It exploded in a mini-fireball that rocked the gate, knocking Helen and Enola off balance. They toppled off the walkway.

The child screamed.

Then Helen was hanging by both hands from the edge of the walkway, with the child clinging to her. They swayed there precariously as smoke rose from the explosion below.

As the smoke cleared, the Mariner could see that the bottom half of the gate had been blasted apart. Not big enough a hole to sail through, but he cruised toward it anyway. He ran into it, letting his mast bump jarringly up to a halt against the upper remaining portion.

Then he climbed up the mast and leapt onto the catwalk.

"Thank heaven!" Helen gasped, the child dangling around her neck like a human necklace.

But he jumped over where Helen's fingertips clung to the edge of the catwalk. He ran along the walkway to the open gate tower. He found the right lever, and the gate—or what was left of it—began to swing slowly, rumblingly open.

Then he ran down the moving rampway, toward the dangling Helen and Enola. He leapt over them and threw himself at the trimaran mast, sliding down the pole onto the ship.

Helen screamed at him, furious.

But he was already at the helm, guiding his ship into the rain of water-cannon mist.

The sail *whump*ed as Helen and Enola dropped from the catwalk onto the full, passing sail of the trimaran. They came sliding down, landing on the netting deck, in a pile.

Helen glared at the Mariner. He just looked at her, then steered the boat out into the open sea.

The Mariner was pleased to see that the Smoker's gunboat was behind them. The gunboat's massive weapon was aimed at an atoll wall.

But he was not pleased to see another craft before them: a sprawling barge where jetskis and small boats were refueling. The deck was littered with Smokers.

And now the gunboat was starting to turn, its massive gun still spitting death. The Mariner turned to Helen.

"Steer for me," he told her.

"Why should I trust you?" she asked him, glaring.

He grabbed a line and swung out to the bow harpoon station. Drawing a careful bead on the gunboat, he fired.

The harpoon caught the gunboat in the bow, and the harpoon line drew taut.

The trimaran had a catch.

Soon the Mariner's boat was towing the gunboat, pulling it and its careening crew around. Its massive gun was shooting up the ocean.

Then the gunboat hit an unintended target. Its gunfire tore into the refueling barge's bow, and the barge detonated like the floating bomb it was. It disappeared in a startling fireball as its crew leapt overboard.

On the trimaran, the Mariner cut the harpoon line, then returned to the helm. His ship sailed through the rain of fiery debris and a fog of smoke.

Soon the smoke began to thin and clear.

5

The trimaran, despite its battered condition, was sailing smoothly. With a spare sail in hand, the Mariner dove from the ship into the icy waters. He swam under the main hull to plug up a hole blown there in the battle.

That should hold her—for now.

Soon he was flopping back onto the trimaran deck, dripping wet. He reached for his plastic bottle of murky water and swigged, once.

Helen sat nervously beside the mast with its broken lines and tattered sail swinging just above her.

"I know what you're thinking," she said.

He said nothing. Instead, he glanced at the child, who sat silently on the stern. She was staring across the sea back in the direction they'd come, her face blank with shock. He felt bad for her.

"You're thinking," she said, "how much longer that hydro of yours would last, if there weren't three of us on this boat."

He screwed the cap back on the water bottle.

"Well, Enola won't drink much, and I won't drink at all," she said. "Not till we get there."

He frowned. "Get where?"

"Wherever you got your dirt."

"I salvaged it off an atoll the Smokers hit."

"Smokers don't leave anything behind after a raid—*especially* dirt."

He said nothing.

"You've been there, haven't you?" she said. Her voice was hushed. "*Dryland* . . . you know where it is."

"Sure. I know where it is."

"I *knew* it," she said. "And we . . . we're going there?"

"*I* am."

"We saved your life! Without us, you wouldn't've got out of there—"

"You got me out," he said, "so you could get out. That makes us even."

She scrambled to her feet. "Look, I can fish . . . I can cook . . ."

"So can I."

Her eyes were flashing with desperate thought. Then her fingers flew to her neck, removing her necklace. She held it out to him.

"Take this, then," she said. "It's worth—"

"You air-breathers are all alike. You know what I

was *really* thinking? Why shouldn't I drop you both in my wake, right now!"

He began working the sails.

Her voice came from behind him, and there was a new edge in it—a harsh edge.

"You're taking us to Dryland. *Both* of us."

He turned slowly and looked at her.

The small speargun was aimed directly for his heart.

While the Mariner and Helen were talking, Enola climbed down inside the cramped cabin. Like any kid, she couldn't resist exploring. Almost immediately she touched a latch that sent a board slamming open.

Jumping back, she cocked an ear, expecting the sound to attract the grown-ups' attention, and get her a scolding.

The piece of wood that fell from the wall made a sort of desk, and on it was pinned a homemade map. There were shelves and square cubbyholes in the space the board had been hiding. And more charts were rolled up, there—paper!

And in one of the cubbyholes, she found a box. She could not read the words on it—"Crayola crayons—64 colors"—but she knew at once what the objects were for.

She snatched a crayon labeled "Cyan" and made a test line on one of the water-stained, ancient pieces of

51

paper. But she turned it over to the blank side first. She didn't want to spoil it.

The test line turned out beautifully. She'd never had *color* drawsticks before, and now she could make color pictures!

Wonderful images began to spill out of her: birds, horses, people in their huts, mountains—with shadings of this hue and that one.

"Killing's a hard thing to do well," the Mariner told Helen, still working with the sails. "And, believe me, I'm not the one to start on."

But her expression was determined, and the tiny speargun in her hand was steady.

"Maybe you wouldn't be the first man I killed," she said.

He shoved the tiller hard over, making the boat point sharply up. The sail billowed aft, smothering the woman within its canvas blanket.

He grabbed a boat oar and thumped the lump in the sail's middle—her head—with one good hard whack.

The lump slumped.

Then he reached under the canvas and yanked the speargun from her limp hand.

Now maybe he could concentrate on sailing, and make a little time before those Smokers came looking for them.

*   *   *

By the next day, the trimaran was shipshape, or as close to it as could be expected. Spliced lines sped through pulleys, frazzled sails snapped shut.

He sat on deck, drinking from a jug of hydro when Helen sheepishly approached him.

"Can I have some?" she asked. "It's not for me. It's for the girl."

He handed her the hydro jug, and watched her cross to where Enola sat near the mast. Helen knelt by the child, smiled and made her drink all of the water.

At least she kept her word, the Mariner noted. *Didn't take any for herself.*

Enola's voice was soft, and intended for Helen. "Is he taking us to Dryland?"

Helen said, "Yeah. He is."

He spliced the torn dragline, biting the rope to test its strength. It would hold. Then he sat, coiling the rope.

The child came slowly across the springy netting deck. Her face was solemn, her braids swinging in the breeze.

"Thank you for saving us."

She bent forward and kissed him on the cheek.

He couldn't have been more surprised—or unnerved—if she had struck him. He moved quickly away from the child, finding the farthest corner of his boat, to be as far away from them as possible.

53

"Just stay away from him," he heard Helen advise Enola.

He took his seat at the console and plucked his telescope from its scabbard. He began slowly scanning the horizon. Then something was blocking his sights.

"For the love of Poseidon!" he swore at the girl. "You're in my view!"

"Enola!" Helen called. "Get over here!"

At least the child was quick to obey.

But as she scurried away, he noticed something clutched in her hand—one of his crayons.

Had she been in his things?

Grimacing with irritation, he turned to complain to Helen, but then noticed something else.

Drawings—right on the hull! Sketches of Smokers and Atollers in battle . . .

The child was sitting, using the Crayola to scribble more images onto the central hull.

He stalked over to her. "What do you think you're doing?"

She didn't look up at him. "Decorating your boat. It's ugly."

He picked her up—she almost flew out of his hands, she was so light—and set her aside roughly. Then he snatched the Crayola from her hand, found a cloth, and knelt and rubbed at the drawings. And rubbed.

They didn't come off.

He stood, tossing the cloth to his feet. He shook a

scolding finger at her. "You don't touch *anything* of mine."

She looked up at him, her eyes wide and deep and very blue. "I drew it for you."

He bent over and shook a fist at her. "You don't draw on *anything* of mine. Understand?"

She was expressionless, and not at all frightened.

Exasperated, he shook his head—and something else caught his eye. The nearby sail was covered with Crayola drawings.

"You take up space," he snarled at the child, "and you slow me down!"

"She doesn't know the rules," Helen said.

He hadn't seen her approach. It was as if she were a guardian angel suddenly hovering over the child.

"You two want to stay?" he asked.

Helen, a hand on the girl's shoulder, swallowed hard, and nodded.

"Then teach her," he said, and he went to the tiller.

Again, he heard the woman's warning to the child: "Stay away from him."

But not five minutes later, there the child was, standing looking at him.

"How many men have you killed?" she asked.

He didn't answer.

"Ten?"

He didn't answer.

"Twenty?"

55

"You talk too much," he said.

"I talk too much," she said, "'cause you don't talk enough . . . How many have you killed?"

"You mean, including children?"

She studied him, trying to figure out if he was kidding her or if it was a threat.

Then she said, "I'm not afraid of you. I told Helen you wouldn't be so ugly if you cut off some of that hair."

That did it.

He scooped her up and said, "You talk all the time, it's like a storm when you're around," and he heaved the wide-eyed girl over the side.

The splash alerted Helen. She looked over the side at the girl, thrashing in the sea, and yelled, "She can't swim!"

And then the woman dove in after the child.

Shaking his head, he headed aft, to bring the ship around to pick them up. Helen swam well and had the child in tow. He had to admire her spirit, jumping in like that.

A *pop* caught his attention. He swung his face above the swimming woman, looking to the horizon.

Then he heard another backfiring-like *pop*.

He had meant to help the woman back up into the boat, but then she was boosting Enola up on deck. Helen was wringing wet, and hopping mad.

"If you ever touch that child again," she began.

His eyes searched the opposite horizon. Not a boat in sight . . .

There was a droning sound, not unlike the mechanical drone that announced the speedboats and jetskis of . . .

"Smokers?" Helen asked.

He turned his attention to the sky.

Engine missing, buzz-sawing over the water, spewing smoke, the battered seaplane loped into view. Then it looped in and began circling the trimaran.

"Can we outrun him?" Helen asked.

"Not with my sails down," the Mariner said. "They may not open fire. They're just scouting us."

The plane circled them, then swooped down toward the bow. As it came around, they could see a goggled tailgunner aiming a machine gun their way. The machine gun barked at them, bullets stitching their way across the water.

The three of them ran for the main cabin. The roar of the seaplane engine told them the plane was coming around for another try at them.

Enola ducked behind the mast, Helen right behind her. But the Mariner stopped in his tracks, and quickly ran toward the rear of the ship, diving down a hatch.

Over the seaplane's rumble, he could hear the woman's shout, "Hey!"

But he had disappeared below deck not to hide, rather to arm himself. He snatched a double-barreled speargun off the bulkhead. He whipped out his knife, sliced the line connecting spears and gun, and leapt back up onto the hull.

The machine gun was silent, though the plane was swooping in for another try.

Helen had positioned herself at the harpoon gun mounted on the bow. She was swinging the big weapon around, taking aim at the circling plane.

Her face was tight with determination and he admired her courage, even as he screamed, "*Nooooooo . . . !*"

She fired the gun. Its big harpoon streaked into the sky, trailing its line. Just as the gunner was swinging his machine gun around, the harpoon stabbed through the plane's fuselage.

The tailgunner slumped over the now useless gun. Helen hadn't just skewered the plane, with her shot— she'd hit the gunner, as well.

The pilot was looking back frantically at his silenced gunner and at his wounded plane.

Only the plane wasn't just wounded; it was harpooned like an airborne whale.

And as the plane flew, the line connecting it to the harpoon gun began to tighten. Helen's face showed her dawning horror, as she realized what she'd done.

Knife in hand, the Mariner ran toward the bow, even as the ship lurched with the plane fighting the restraining line. The deck around the harpoon gun began to groan like an injured beast.

Then the entire harpoon gun and its stand ripped free of the deck, and went flying over his head.

Like a fish that had taken bait from the sky, the harpoon gun rode its line upward. It shredded sails and lines as it went.

Soon it was caught above, the line wrapped around the mast.

The double-barreled speargun was on a strap, so he tossed it around his shoulder, stuck his knife in his teeth, and began climbing the teetering pole.

The higher up he got, the more nauseating the sway of the mast was. The plane was yanking the boat from side to side. But he was nearing where he could get at that vibrating harpoon line and cut the trimaran free.

A bullet tore through the sail next to him. Not from the machine gun, but something smaller: a pistol!

He grabbed a line, swung out from the mast and yanked his speargun off his shoulder. Drawing a bead on the plane, he sent a spear winging . . .

Four pistol shots stitched across the sail next to him, and as he ducked the bullets, his knife slipped from his hand. It went tumbling, then clattering, to the deck.

He still had one spear in the speargun. He leaned out and took careful aim as the plane closed in on him.

He could see the pilot leaning out, pistol in hand. The Mariner took aim . . .

But the pilot shot first.

The shot wasn't aimed at the Mariner, but at the harpoon rope that bound the plane to his boat. The Smoker plane lurched free, and the remains of the rope fluttered after it.

The recoiling mast tossed the Mariner backward, through the tattered trimaran sails, into midair. Finally, it dropped him in the water as if he were an engine that fell off the retreating plane.

He was underwater when the harpoon gun and stand fell to the deck and crashed through it. When he bobbed to the surface, he was so hot with anger, it was a wonder that the water around him didn't boil.

He swam quickly to the boat and hauled himself aboard.

He glanced around his ship. It looked like a typhoon had hit.

He glared at the woman. She stood sheepishly, the child cowering behind her.

"I'm sorry," Helen said. "I was just trying to—"

"The next time you touch anything on my boat," he said, "I'll toss you both in the water and leave you there."

He stepped around them and tried to find some corner of the boat where he could be alone for a while, before he once again began repairing his home.

The Mariner (Kevin Costner), Helen (Jeanne Tripplehorn), and Enola (Tina Majorino) face adventure and adversity on the endless seas of Waterworld.

The mysterious child Enola holds the key to Waterworld's most treasured secret.

The Mariner's trimaran glides into the lagoon of Oasis atoll.

The set for *Waterworld*'s Oasis atoll is one of the most elaborate in moviemaking history.

A music box plays a haunting tune with meaning to Enola.

Enola tries to make friends with the hard-bitten captain of the trimaran.

Are the strange markings on Enola's back a map to Dryland?

The Mariner's lonely life at sea is changed forever by the events in *Waterworld*.

Are Enola's doodlings the visions of an imaginative child or memories of early days in Dryland?

The Mariner has never met anyone who can't swim before—so he gives Enola a lesson.

Enola doesn't cooperate with her pirate
host, the evil Deacon (Dennis Hopper).

When the Deacon's Smokers attack the atoll, Helen
and Enola rush to defend their home.

Vicious Smokers assault the peaceful atoll on their powerful jetskis.

6

The trimaran sailed easily in a whisper of west-southeast wind. Helen sat next to a daydreaming Enola. The Mariner was rigging his newly patched sails. Then he moved to his steering console.

Enola's stomach growled.

Helen looked toward the Mariner. He stood so still, he might have been carved there.

She went over to him. "Please . . . if you'd just give me something to fish with, I'll catch them myself."

"Not in these waters," he said.

"What?"

He looked away from her.

"We're hungry," she said. "The child is hungry."

"You don't understand."

"What don't I understand?"

"What fishing is like, around here."

From behind them, Enola's voice chimed, "Maybe he doesn't know how to fish."

He shook his head and stormed away, leaping into the recess of the cabin in the main hull.

For a few moments, Helen thought he was just trying to get away from them. But then clattering below deck told them he was up to something.

He emerged with a strange-looking two-headed harpoon gun. Eyes burning, he fastened a long coil of rusty wire to his trawling mechanism.

Enola was at Helen's side. "What's he doing, Helen?"

"I'm not sure."

Now he was securing the other end of the wire around the middle of the harpoon gun.

"Should I ask him?" Enola wondered.

"No!" Helen said.

Then the Mariner, harpoon gun clutched in both hands, threw himself off the stern of the slowly moving boat.

Hanging onto the harpoon gun as if it were a handle tied to a ski rope, the Mariner lay face down on the foaming water.

The boat was dragging him!

The Mariner was making strange, dolphinlike squeaks as he skimmed along behind the boat. Kicking expertly, he swung back and forth across the trimaran's wake. Then he began spinning on the end of the wire!

Helen frowned. Like . . . like a fishing lure!

Suddenly a huge blue creature burst into view.

Thirty feet long, with the body of a whale and countless rudderlike fins, it leapt like a dolphin!

Only dolphins didn't have huge jaws ringed with pointy, razor-sharp teeth. . . .

Enola clutched Helen around the waist, and both she and the child gasped. Their eyes were wide and frozen as the beast swallowed the Mariner in one gulp.

The trawling wire snapped.

"No!" the child screamed.

The beast remained on the surface, savoring its meal.

Then a *thunk* emerged from within the beast. A harpoon shot out from the side of its awful head. Then a second *thunk* announced the second harpoon's exit from the other side of its skull.

Soon a knife blade jutted out near the jaws of the dead beast. The Mariner was cutting himself an exit from his catch of the day.

"Oh my," Helen said.

She really *hadn't* understood about fishing in these waters . . .

By late afternoon, Helen was keeping her promise and doing the cooking. Enormous whalephin steaks sizzled on a small grill.

Gentle singing—Enola's—floated on the breeze.

"There is a girl that lives in the wind," she sang,

hanging onto the masts with one arm, "in the wind, in the wind. There is . . ."

The Mariner looked up sharply at the girl.

"Helen says you don't like my singing," the child said, "because you can't sing yourself."

"Enola!" Helen said.

The Mariner said to the girl, "You ever stop and just listen?"

Enola seemed puzzled. "To what?"

"To the music of Waterworld."

The child cocked her head, trying to hear something, then shook her head. "I don't hear anything."

"That's because you're talking all the time," he said. "Try sitting still, for a change."

Enola frowned.

He pushed the water jug toward them with his foot.

Helen reached for the jug. "It's all right . . . we can . . . ?"

"Drink all you want," he said. "It's going to rain tonight."

Enola was staring at the foot that had pushed the jug toward them, staring at his webbed toes.

"I wish I had feet like yours," Enola said.

"Enola!" Helen said.

The Mariner just looked at the child.

"Then maybe I could swim," Enola said.

After supper, a contented Helen curled up for a nap.

Before long, a sound stirred her awake. She pushed

64

up on an elbow. A bloodred sun was setting, turning the sea shades of glimmering crimson and gold. She settled back onto the deck and the sound repeated.

It was a scream! *Enola's* scream!

Helen scrambled to her feet and ran to the side. Out on the crimson-gold water, the Mariner was swimming easily on his back. Enola was gleefully sitting on his chest, riding along.

The screams had been squeals of delight.

"Enola!" Helen yelled. "What are you doing?! Those monsters will kill you!"

"They're asleep now," the Mariner said.

He turned over and swung the child onto his back. She hung on, around his neck.

"No need to be frightened," he was telling her. "Let the water tell you how to move your arms and legs."

For the next hour, Helen watched as their gruff captain gave the child a swimming lesson.

"Look!" Enola said. "Look, Helen!"

It was just a dog-paddle, but it was a start.

Later, on deck, the sea a deep blue under a dark, cloudy sky, she asked the Mariner why he'd done that.

Sitting at the tiller, he shrugged. "I just never met anybody who couldn't swim before."

"I . . . I have something for you," she said.
"What?"

She showed him a sketch Enola had done of the three of them, on the deck of the trimaran together.

"Enola wanted to give you this, but she was afraid to."

He didn't say anything. But then he reached out and took the drawing.

Helen said, "We . . . we wanted to thank you. But we don't even know your name."

"I don't have one."

It was the saddest thing she'd ever heard.

"The marks on her back," he said. "What are they?"

Helen had wondered when they'd get around to this.

"Nothing," she said.

"They must mean something," the Mariner said. "They're not a birthmark. Somebody put them there."

The endless sea was black and charcoal and gray and blue. The wind whispered across its surface: *Trust him . . . you can trust him . . .*

"About six years ago," she said quietly, "a basket floated into Oasis with a child in it. A baby . . . a little girl."

"Enola," he said.

She nodded. "Everyone wanted to push her back out to sea—that was the law of the Elders. But I said I'd take her. There was no one else who wanted her—she would have died otherwise."

"And the marks? They were already on her back?"

Helen nodded.

"What do they mean, these marks?"

She hesitated, then she said, "Old Gregor thinks it charts the way to Dryland."

66

He slumped at the tiller. "Dryland. Dryland's a myth."

"It's not!" she blurted. "You said so yourself, you said you knew where it was, you said you were taking us there—"

"*You* said I was taking you there. Maybe I'm planning to drop you off at the first atoll we stumble on."

She was insistent. "Dryland is real."

He shook his head. "You're a fool, believing in something you've never seen."

"But I *have* seen it. Anyway, I've touched it. I've held dirt far richer and darker than what you traded, back at the atoll."

He looked at her with narrow eyes. "Where?"

"In the basket we found Enola in."

He thought about that, then shook his head, and sighed. Finally he said, "So you want to see Dryland. You *really* want to see it?"

"Of course!"

"Then I'll show it to you tomorrow."

And that was all he'd say.

Trembling with excitement, she left the Mariner at his post, and went to tell Enola it was time for bed.

7

A bell-shaped wire cage bobbed, half-submerged, in the water. Helen watched the Mariner, down in the water, attaching weights. He had already connected a large jellyfish-like membrane to a gas canister. He had also pitched flares into the water, to light their way.

"Get in!" he called to her, from the water.

Enola's wide eyes took all this in. "I want to go, too."

Helen called down to him: "What about the child?"

"There's only air for one," he yelled up.

Trembling with anticipation, Helen splashed in beside the Mariner, bobbing up next to him.

The water was cold, but refreshing, though her body was covered with goosebumps.

"Get in the bell," the Mariner said.

And she dove below. She steered herself up within the wire-mesh framework. Then she found the opening of the air bladder, surfacing inside of it. It began to balloon around her. Suddenly she was encased in a bubble . . . and there was air to breathe!

She could see him out there. He needed no breathing apparatus except the gills behind his ears. His hair streaming as he swam in place, he mouthed the word "Okay?"

Within her transparent cocoon, she gave him a thumbs-up sign.

Now the whole rig came dropping down, further and further below the surface.

The Mariner clutched the wire-mesh, riding along on the downward journey. Inside her transparent bubble, Helen looked out as jellyfish and other sea denizens swam across her line of vision. Some of them glided, others seemed to crawl. Their colors put the drab blues and browns and grays of Waterworld to shame.

The rig dropped to a depth where the sunlight no longer could filter down its rays. But blossoms of rose-colored light were just below them. The Mariner's flares were charting a course for them.

Still falling, the rig overtook the flares, and they entered a murky twilight. What did this have to do with Dryland? Nowhere in Waterworld could be wetter!

And then the cage rocked to a stop, a landing softened by their water-cushioned fall. Something solid! The cage was resting on something dark, something hard.

Before long, the flares caught up with them, bringing artificial rose-hued dawn to a breathtaking vista.

It was the wondrously jagged underwater skyline of a centuries-old city!

And Helen—in her bubble, in her cage—was at the edge of a rooftop. Skyscrapers no longer scraped the sky, but reached like square stone fingers into the ocean above.

Then the Mariner tugged her cage off the roof.

And now they tumbled down, plunging past crumbling window frames. How incredibly tall these structures had been! The atoll's windmill had seemed towering. Here, it would have been a toy.

With a water-cushioned clang, the cage landed at street level. Seaweed danced before a huge bank building. Moray eels swam in and out of the glassless windows of a bus. Streetlamps stood, draped with kelp. Cars sat rusted and encrusted. In a store window, an unclothed female mannequin wore a necklace of diamonds and barnacles.

The Mariner scooped some mud off the ocean floor. He cupped both hands full of it. Then he showed her, displayed for her, his precious dirt.

And within Helen, her dream of Dryland died.

Soon, the Mariner was helping the dejected Helen back onto the ship.

"I . . . didn't know," she said, shaking, shaken.

"All this time I didn't know there were . . . *cities* down there."

"Nobody knows," he told her. "But me. And now you."

That was when he saw them—Smoker boats, in the water, ringing the trimaran.

There was no sign of Enola. There were no Smokers on the decks. But the rusted Smoker boats were everywhere, surrounding them.

Now Helen saw them, too, and clutched his arm.

"Can you get us out of here?" she whispered.

A commanding voice from below deck bellowed a response: "I'd say there are two chances of that. No way, and no how!"

And a Smoker stepped from the cabin.

He was not just any Smoker, but a grand commanding chief Smoker. He was bald, sunburned, and wore an eye patch. His tattered uniform hung on him like seaweed.

And he was smiling. Grinning.

Two more Smokers emerged from the cabin. One of them was the blond, cruel-featured Nord.

"Shoulda brought me that drink, Dirt Man," the Nord said.

Smokers began filling the decks of the encircling boats.

The Smoker chieftain swaggered up to the Mariner and Helen.

72

"Proper introductions, first," he said. "I'm the Deacon."

It was a name the Mariner was all too familiar with. A name all Waterworld knew and, for the most part, feared.

"I've come for the child with the markings on her back," the Deacon said. "I suspect she's somewhere close . . ."

So did the Mariner. He figured she had ducked down into the crossarm hatch. Enola often went there to be alone.

"We *could* tear the boat apart looking for her," the Deacon said.

Then the Smoker chieftain held out two open palms. The Nord placed a handgun in each.

The Deacon pointed one gun at the Mariner, and the other at Helen.

"If you don't tell me where the girl is," the Deacon said to the Mariner, "I swear to Poseidon I'll torch your boat."

The Mariner looked at Helen and she stared back at him. And in that moment, they forged a bond, no less strong for being unspoken.

"All right," the Deacon said, and he raised one of the guns. "If they won't tell us where the kid is, we'll just kill *both* of them."

And the Deacon fired the gun upward, twice.

The Mariner winced, knowing what the result would be.

Enola came scrambling up out of the crossarm hatch, screaming, "No! No!"

Her distressed expression turned joyful, as she saw the Mariner and Helen still alive. But then her face melted back into gloom.

"Oh, so gullible, these children," the Deacon said. "But I do dearly love the innocent little brats. Bring her here."

The Smoker guard grabbed the child as if she were an object, and carried her to the Deacon.

The Deacon tugged at the child's tunic to reveal the tattoo. "That mean anything to you?" the Deacon asked the Nord.

"No."

"I can't cipher it out, either. We'll do it back on the *'Deez*."

The Nord glanced toward the Mariner and Helen. "What about them?"

"Kill them both."

"And the boat?"

"Torch it."

In one swift motion, the Mariner grabbed Helen by the wrist and yanked her along, running to the bow.

Then he dove over the side, pulling Helen in with him, the Nord's gunfire drilling the water as they plunged down.

74

His hand gripped her wrist, guiding her. Helen followed his lead under the water. They swam deeper, and deeper, as bullets chased them down, not catching them. Slowed by the water, the bullets were sinking harmlessly around them like little lead weights.

But then her air, bubbling away in increasingly smaller trails, began to give out.

I'm drowning, she thought. *Heaven help me, I'm drowning!*

The Mariner stopped, treading underwater, and drew Helen to him.

It was as if he were kissing her, but it was a kiss of life as he shared air with her.

Calmed, she allowed him to loop an arm around her waist and they went swimming away, together. Deep under the water, kicking in tandem, they were like a fish school of two. They would pause, now and then, for the Mariner to share his air with her.

Perhaps an hour later, they surfaced far away from the trimaran. It was only a dot on the horizon. But they could see the telltale trail of smoke curling like an awful question mark into the sky.

They could see, too, the Smoker boats pulling away in triumph.

"We have to go back," Helen said.

The Mariner nodded, bobbing next to her. "We can start now . . . we'll be there by sunset."

And they were. They traveled the last leg of their

75

homeward journey underwater again. Then they surfaced cautiously, not knowing whether a Smoker guard had been left behind.

Before them was the smoldering hulk of the once-proud trimaran.

They swam to the wreck and climbed aboard. No sign of the girl.

Then Helen saw the box of crayons, its contents a swirl of melted colors on the scorched hull.

She watched the Mariner as he walked with slumped shoulders, a dejected ghost haunting the ruins of his own house.

"Check below deck," she said.

He nodded, and went.

A breeze stirred the seared remnants of the trimaran. She could almost hear the song Enola used to sing: *There is a girl that lives in the wind, in the wind, in the wind . . .*

He came up from below, shaking his head no. "No sign of her," he said.

"I can't go on," she said, falling to her knees. Her fingers drifted across the melted blur of crayon colors on the hull. And she began to weep.

"I miss the sound of her . . . her singing," she said. "Do you?"

He looked away. "I miss my boat."

This didn't strike her as a cold thing for him to say so much as a sad thing.

"You know," Helen said, "you're so much better at being alone than I am."

He crouched beside her.

"I was born on an atoll," he told her quietly. It was a whisper that almost got lost in the wind. "People wanted to kill me. I was a freak."

She touched his arm.

"My mother taught me to read, but she died young. Some, when they're beaten down, get stronger . . ."

He was talking about himself, she knew.

"My father kept me alive to dive after fish," he said. "Kept me on a lead line."

"What?"

"He knew if he didn't, I'd never come back. So I stole his boat. And I've been on one boat or another, ever since."

"How old were you?"

"Enola's age," he said. "Maybe a little older."

"Enola knew what it was like to be different," she said. "I think that's why she liked you."

She leaned forward and, very tenderly, kissed him. "You were kind, to teach Enola to swim," she said. Sunset was turning the sea crimson and gold; it was as if the ocean had caught fire. The trimaran was like a stray floating ember.

And they sat there together, rekindling hope in each other's arms.

77

By the following afternoon, they had constructed a raft from the rubble of the ship. Then they set out to sea. They closed their eyes and waited for the wind to decide which way to take them.

"*Helen . . .*" a voice called, echoing over the water.

Her eyes fluttered open and she looked into the puzzled gaze of the Mariner.

"*Is that you . . . ?*"

Their eyes searched the sea, but then, seeing nothing, they shrugged at each other. Who was talking to them?

"*No, no, no . . . up here!*"

And then drifting into view, just above them, was the cigar-shaped dirigible with its quilt-work balloon! Sitting in his chair, controlling his airship, was Old Gregor.

Helen sprang to her feet, making the raft sway. "Gregor!"

"Smart thinking, burning your boat," the old man said. It was as casual as if the last time they'd seen each other was over breakfast. "I never would have seen you if not for the smoke. Who's that with you?"

The Mariner was on his feet, too, sizing up their hovering visitor.

"Why, it's Ichthyus Sapien!" Gregor said. Delight lighted up his white-bearded countenance.

Helen cried, "What're you doing here?"

"Looking for survivors from the atoll attack," he said. "The rest of us are on the Eastern banks." Gregor was moving in closer. "This is a true miracle! Here, grab hold . . . I'll lower some lines and pull you on."

Soon they were climbing up into the dirigible seats that had been designed for Helen and Enola.

And this finally prompted the absent-minded inventor to ask, "Oh, dear . . . the child! Where is Enola?"

"Smokers took her," Helen said forlornly. She nodded toward the Mariner. "They'd have *me*, too, if it hadn't been for him."

The Mariner was nervous, sitting in a boat that rode the sky, not the sea. He looked down toward his ruined trimaran.

"Very human of you," Gregor said.

And they sailed away in the sky.

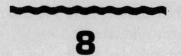

8

Dots along the horizon gradually became a ragtag cluster of boats. Rafted together, with gangways between them, the boats formed a new atoll. The survivors of the Smoker raid on Oasis had banded together, rebuilding, beginning anew.

Helen turned in her seat and saw the Mariner's uneasy expression. He sat gripping the arms of his seat.

"Are you all right?" Helen asked him.

"I should've stayed with the raft."

"They won't try to harm you," she said. "They'll be grateful. They'll welcome you, just like Gregor did. . . ."

The wind was ruffling his hair. She could see both the shell earring and the gills.

"Last time," he said, "they welcomed me into their organo barge."

"I'll tell them how you saved my life—"

He was shaking his head, no. "I don't want to stay. I just want a boat."

She searched his face. "Will you take me with you?"

"Is that what *you* want?"

"I want to talk the Atollers into going after the Smokers . . . going after Enola . . ."

He looked at her a long time. "They won't do it."

Stubbornly, she said, "They may."

"She may already be dead."

"I know. But I have to try."

And the balloon dipped, as Old Gregor guided it toward the ramshackle assembly of boats.

Before long, dusk was turning the fishing trawlers of New Oasis into silhouettes against the copper sky. Smaller boats dotted the water, ashimmer with gold.

On the deck of a beat-up trawler, the Mariner sat by himself, eating a bowl of mush. Within the trawler, a meeting was being held. His fate was being decided. Once again, he had not been invited to his own trial.

Within the trawler, Helen stood at the window, staring out at the lonely figure of the Mariner. Behind her the Atollers bickered and ranted.

"It's not *safe* to leave him unchained out there!" an atoller man was shouting.

A woman said, "He's right! We have children here!"

Helen turned away from the window to face the group. Some sat at tables, others stood. Fear was in every face but Old Gregor's. He sat on a bench in front, his smile comforting, his nods quietly cheering her on.

"You needn't bother figuring out what to do about him," Helen said. "He's leaving."

"How?" another Atoller man said.

"On one of *our* boats?" demanded another.

She shrugged. "You can give him one . . . or he'll just take one. Your choice."

The brawny figure of the Enforcer moved through the group like a parent among small children. "He's earned that much. And he's free to leave."

There were murmurings, but not very loud. The Enforcer's word was law, here.

"We have a decision to make," the Enforcer said. "Helen has asked that we untie our boats, and set out for the child."

"She's among Smokers!" someone said.

"Let's hear her out," the Enforcer said. "Helen— please speak."

"The world wasn't created in the Great Deluge," Helen said. Eyes around the room went immediately wide at this blasphemy. "The land was not washed away—it was *covered* by it."

A woman from the back chimed out shrilly, "The Elders say—"

"They say nothing," Helen clipped her off. "They're dead. I'm alive, and I have seen it with my own eyes. There are cities down there—dead ones, but they were once alive."

83

The murmurings were louder now, and the Enforcer silenced them. "Quiet! Helen, go on . . ."

She did. "If there's land down there, that means there could be land *above* water, too . . . somewhere on the horizon."

Now there were laughs. "Where, then?"

Another voice scoffed, "What heading? How far?"

"My friends," Old Gregor said in a booming voice, "listen to me. I'm convinced Enola carries the way to Dryland on her back."

Another Atoller stood. "Do we have to listen to this nonsense? Dryland's a hoax—we decided that years ago."

Heads were nodding. The Enforcer stood to take the vote.

But Helen knew, even before the show of hands, what the outcome would be.

On deck, the Mariner was preparing the trawler to get underway. He would need better sails, and it would take months of salvage work down in the dead cities, to gather the necessary barter to . . .

And she was standing beside him.

Her expression was grim. "They're not going after her."

"What did you expect?"

She sighed, shook her head. "You have to understand, they're afraid. They're only human . . ."

"I don't understand people, human or otherwise, who won't go after their own kind."

Her hand settled on his shoulder. "Will you go after her?"

"No."

Her hand fell away. Dusk was blending into night. There were no streetlamps in New Oasis. Perhaps the old inventor would build them a new windmill for the Smokers to come and burn down.

"Enola said you were her friend," Helen said.

It was as if she had slapped him. The sensation puzzled him.

But he shrugged it off and went back to coiling the rope.

Helen's voice trembled as she said, quietly, "What do I tell her when I see her again?"

What was there to say to that? Hadn't he told the woman that the child was probably dead? He turned his back to her and went about doing his best to get this sorry tub shipshape.

He didn't see her step off the trawler, onto the deck.

And later, when he guided the trawler away from the atoll, he didn't notice that Helen and Old Gregor were on the dock, watching him go.

Enola was cold, and she was afraid. She was inside a cell, chained to a bare metal bunk in a bare metal cell, huddled on the bare metal floor.

85

She missed Helen. She missed the Mariner. She thought of his wonderful boat and remembered the awful sight of it on fire, flames licking the sails, turning them black.

And she cried.

Suddenly the door to the little cell swung open. The Deacon stepped in, with the mean blond Nord following him.

"What's the meaning of this?" the Deacon demanded. "Take these chains off the child! Are we savages here?"

The Nord removed the chain from her ankle.

"There," the Deacon said. "Isn't that better?"

Enola said nothing.

"Sit up on the bunk, now, with me. Take my hand."

Reluctantly, she took his hand. It was surprisingly soft, as it guided her next to him on the metal bunk.

"How would you like this, dear?" he asked.

And he opened his hand to reveal her crayon.

A Smoker had pried it from her fingers, on the trimaran. She thought it was long gone. How dearly she wanted it back! She could decorate these horrible bare walls . . .

But she just gazed at him, eyes big and unblinking. She thought about how the Mariner would behave if he were this terrible man's prisoner.

"It's yours," the Deacon said, "if you can help me."

She said nothing.

86

"I'm told the tattoo on your back is actually a map of some kind."

She nodded. "It's the way to Dryland, Gregor says."

"By any chance, could you, uh . . . tell me how to read this map?"

She shook her head, no.

"Well, did your friends ever say anything about it? Your mommy, or that big pet fish of yours?"

"Helen isn't my mommy," Enola said, "and you shouldn't make fun of my friend. He wouldn't like it."

The Deacon blinked. "Girl, I lost an eye when that fish-man blew up my boat." Rage colored his voice. "If I ever see him again—"

"You can't kill him."

That seemed to amuse him. "Really? Why not?"

She shrugged. "'Cause he's fast, and he's strong, like a big wind. And he's even meaner than you are."

The Deacon frowned. "There's not a man alive who can make that claim."

She shrugged again. "He's not a man."

The Deacon patted her gently on the head. "Well, I'm glad we had the chance to have this little talk. Nord, chain the brat!"

Then he stormed from the room.

The Nord refastened the chain. Enola huddled against the wall, whispering to herself.

"He'll come and find me," she said. "He'll take me away. He'll find me . . ."

The door clanged shut.

87

*   *   *

The Mariner had returned to the burnt-out shell of his trimaran to salvage tools and weapons from the ship's cubbyholes.

Right now, he was in the charred remains of his cabin, sitting on the scorched bunk. He was looking at a chart the looting Smokers had missed. He'd found a crayon, as well.

He made a dot on the chart and wrote the word "Denver." That was the drowned city he and Helen had visited, not so long ago. On this chart were other dots, labelled with the names of other long-dead cities: Seattle, Rio, Flint . . .

For years now, he had been keeping track of the cities below, to better understand his world. And his world was *more* than Waterworld—it was that under-sea kingdom below . . .

But today, in the cabin of his lonely, roasted wreck of a ship, something nagged him.

He went back to his cubbyholes, and found an ancient, weathered map. As he had many times before, he checked it against his homemade chart, and he frowned.

But then he smiled.

The addition of "Denver" had suddenly brought everything into focus.

Stunned by this new knowledge, he absently turned

over his homemade chart to roll it up. That was when he noticed Enola's drawings there.

The trimaran in sailing mode.

Helen with her hair blowing.

The Mariner tossing Enola in the drink.

The whalephin, leaping from the water.

He and Enola swimming.

He traced the simple yet eloquent lines of artwork with a gentle fingertip. Then his tender expression hardened. When he stepped onto the deck, he knew what he had to do.

The wind rushed up, ruffling his hair, exposing his gills, urging him on.

9

The blast startled Helen awake.

She instinctively reached for Enola, who, of course, wasn't there. She sprang from her cot in the cabin of the leaky old scow where she and Old Gregor had been given shelter.

Gregor was awake, too. She could hear him up on deck where he'd been sleeping, stirring noisily. She could hear others, in the atoll, clambering onto their boats.

And soon they were all looking out into an eerily beautiful moonlit night. The water was a glistening textured ivory, fouled by a pair of oil-leaking jetskis straddled by Smokers.

One was plump, the other skinny; both were hairy and unkempt. They were bobbing on their idling machines. The skinny one's smoking jetski had a trail of oil behind it like a black ribbon stretching to the horizon.

The plump one had fired the shot. His smoking shotgun, held in one hand, was aimed at the moon.

The Enforcer stood on the deck of a trawler at the entry to the small lagoon of New Oasis. "Everyone stay quiet!"

The two jetskis chugged noisily, as the Smokers floated there. They were looking at each other, laughing. Like a couple of naughty children.

"What do you want?" the Enforcer demanded of them.

"All *kinds* of things," the plump one said. "But we'll settle for everything you got. Ain't that right, Bone?"

Bone, the skinny one, giggled his reply: "Right, Chester!"

Chester, the plump Smoker, was the brains of this outfit. He holstered his shotgun in a scabbard alongside the jetski. "We're waiting," he said, crossing his powerful arms.

"Why don't you come on up," the Enforcer snarled, "and see what you get?"

Chester snorted a laugh, floating and bobbing. "Doesn't work that way. You don't want to cooperate, fine. We'll go back and get our friends. Ain't that right, Bone?"

But Bone didn't reply.

Bone's jetski was floating, unattended.

Puzzled, the chubby Smoker reached for his shotgun

in its scabbard, and the Mariner flew from the water, tackling him, dragging him down under.

The splashing was ferocious, limbs flashing out, then disappearing. Then the waters stilled.

Swimming gracefully, the Mariner stroked to the nearest boat. Several Atollers—who suddenly seemed very glad to see this "mute-o"—eased him onto the deck. He went to Helen.

"You came back," she said, her face risking a smile.

"I'm going after the child," he said simply.

The Mariner's shabby trawler was docked alongside Helen's scow. Chester's jetski was tied up nearby. On the dock, the Mariner was filling ancient glass bottles with oil. Then he would stuff rags in them.

Old Gregor was helping him.

The Mariner said, "I know what the picture was."

"What picture?" Gregor frowned, then brightened. "Oh! The one I showed you! In the organo-barge cage!"

The Mariner nodded.

Gregor was trembling with excitement. "Is it a map? I always *thought* it was, with longitude and latitude, but—"

"It is a map," the Mariner said. "But it's upside down."

"Upside . . . ?"

"Down," the Mariner completed.

93

"The world . . ." The old man's brow was knit in deepest thought. "Could the poles have . . . reversed?"

"You're the scientist."

"How could you know these things?"

The Mariner nodded toward the sea. "I've been charting the cities below."

"What a wonderful idea!" the old man said. "And you're sure Enola's map is upside down? Oh. Oh. Oh my! This is wonderful!"

"Hand me that rag."

"Is that why you're going after Enola? So you can find Dryland?"

"I don't care about that," the Mariner said.

"No, of course not. It's the child you care about . . . not that you'd ever admit it."

The Mariner glared at him.

"But what you've told me," Gregor said, overwhelmed, his voice hushed, "it's worth so much. I . . . I don't know what to say . . ."

"Good," the Mariner said.

Gregor laughed. It was a rich laugh, and the Mariner had to work at it—a little—not to smile.

Helen approached them. "I'm going with you."

The Mariner took a moment before he replied. "It's easiest if I go alone."

Several Atollers were approaching. They seemed to be a small, self-appointed committee.

The leader said, "This is foolish, going after the Smokers. It's dangerous. Why make trouble?"

"You don't even know which direction they came from," another Atoller said.

The Mariner withdrew from his pocket the little round lighter. He flicked a flame to life, then ignited the strip of cloth in the latest bottle he'd filled. He lobbed the flame-streaking bottle over at Bone's bobbing, unattended jetski.

The bottle smashed and the jetski ignited.

The explosion was a fireball that made the nighttime momentarily day. The Atollers on the dock yelped in surprise, covering their eyes at the harshness of the blast.

Then they were all watching as the trail of oil behind the jetski caught fire. Flames went streaking, shooting back, all the way to the horizon, lighting the Mariner's way.

He looked at Helen. "If Enola's alive, I'll bring her back to you."

Then he loaded the bottle bombs onto the remaining jetski, and mounted it. Turning it around, he headed off in the direction the flame trail pointed.

He only hoped the jetski's go-juice supply would hold out. He kept his eyes glued to the horizon, waiting to find out just what secret place the Smokers skulked off to, after their vicious atoll raids.

Finally, a dawn as fiery as the trail he chased gave

way to a foggy morning. The path of flames seemed shorter, now, getting eaten up in the mist. But voices and clatter and vague shapes were emerging from the distance.

Suddenly, there it was, knifing through the fog, rising before him like a great sea beast!

A ship!

The biggest ship he—or anyone in Waterworld— had ever seen! The ancient vessel was taller than ten of Old Gregor's windmills, a steel monster encrusted with barnacles and rust.

He cut his engine and jumped from the bobbing jetski onto a shelf of barnacles at the ship's base. He began to climb, finding rusted-out holes for his hands and feet.

An engine purred way above, like an insect buzzing. This ship was stationary, more or less. What engine was that, droning up there? He shrugged it off, and kept scaling the rusty slope. Finally he reached the top, fingers clutching the steel lip.

He peeked over.

And every Smoker in Waterworld rushed at him, charging him, screaming.

Confused, frightened, he ducked back down, wondering how his secret assault could have been discovered.

But though the screaming continued, no Smokers reached over to yank him aboard.

He was just hanging there, their screams getting louder, the engine noise above getting louder, too.

Then he noticed a rusted-out hole in the bow that allowed him to peek through. He could now see Smokers—perhaps a hundred of them, or even more—fanning out to either side of the deck. They were in two ungainly groups, pulling a thick heavy rope between them, tight, as if they were playing tug-of-war.

The purring engine sound built into a roar.

The Mariner looked up and saw the same battered seaplane that he and his trimaran had battled. The plane seemed half invisible as it emerged from the fog.

Clutching rust-holes, he clung to the bow, making himself small. The plane swooped down, thundering in, right over the Mariner, and slammed down onto the deck.

Through his peek-hole, the Mariner watched as the plane's undercarriage was snagged by the rope. Smokers grunted and groaned and yelled as they strained to slow the airship.

Then, a few yards from the bridge of the ship, the plane—and its Smoker landing crew—finally came to a screeching stop. The men tumbled and bumped into each other, then whooped with glee.

Another successful Smoker landing.

The sound of another engine caught his attention below. The Mariner looked down at the bobbing jetski, where he'd left it. A small two-Smoker patrol boat pulled up beside it.

He peeked through his rust-hole again. Smokers were dragging a hose toward the now-silent seaplane, refueling it.

Too much activity here—too many Smokers on deck. And only two Smokers below him, in jackets and goggles. One of them had a harpoon rifle in hand, checking out the empty jetski.

The Mariner dropped down between them, grabbing onto them in a double headlock. Then he took them right over the side of their boat and into the water with a splash.

Not long after, the Mariner emerged from the water, alone. He mounted the jetski, wearing the goggles and jacket of a Smoker.

Around the side of the ship, through a giant rust-hole, the Mariner guided the jetski into a launching area for jetskis. He dismounted, passing several Smokers who took him for one of their own.

Through a roughly sawed-out "doorway" that led into the recesses of the ship, the Mariner stepped cautiously. A voice boomed above his head, making the Mariner whirl. He whipped his knife from its sheath.

"*Here he is!*" the voice resounded. It was coming from a small cloth-faced box on the steel wall!

And it continued on: "*The Deacon of the* 'Deez!"

98

Was this box somehow relaying a voice from else-where on the ship?

He sheathed his knife and pressed on, moving deeper into the ship, hoping his Smoker goggles and jacket would pave the way.

But before long, it became obvious some sort of alarm had been sounded. Smoker patrols were rushing down corridors, climbing ladders, drawing weapons. He kept to the shadows, working his way up. All the while those little talking boxes—some positioned high on walls—were emitting the sound of the Smoker leader's voice.

From the cheers that greeted the Deacon's every decree, it was obvious that most of the Smokers were gathered in one place, listening to their leader speak. And that place, logically, would be the deck.

Footsteps on the metal walkway announced company approaching.

Just past the rail, a heavy hanging chain beckoned him. He leaned out—it stretched up at least two walkway levels—and then grabbed hold and started to climb.

The Deacon stood on the bridge of the *'Deez*. Below him the deck was jammed with his loyal men. They were hanging on their leader's every word.

"And a child shall lead them!" the Deacon boomed.

He gestured toward the Nord, who dragged Enola forward.

The Nord turned the girl's back to the audience, and displayed the markings there.

"She is our beacon in the darkness," the Deacon intoned into his microphone. "And she has shown me the *path!*"

The Smokers below bellowed their approval and delight.

"This is the moment we've been waiting for!" the Deacon called. "Get this crate up to speed!"

Down on the deck, Smokers yelled with glee and began firing their pistols into the air. Flare guns sent comets streaking up into the overcast sky.

And then the deck began to empty, as the Deacon's flock ran to take their stations.

Within the *'Deez,* Smokers cascaded down poles, streamed down ladders, ropes, and chains. They scattered here and there.

Outside, cables began to stretch from the looming ship's bow to tugboats whose engines strained under the sheer tonnage of their burden.

But the tugs weren't enough. The vast ship remained motionless. Then, through rusted-out holes from stem to stern, oars extended, paddling through the water.

In the lower level of the *'Deez* sat the ship's willing galley slaves. Smokers everywhere manned massive oars, stroking in perfect unison. And for the first time in centuries, the *Valdez* left port.

On the bridge, the Deacon kept triumphant watch. Smokers were still streaming off deck.

Oozing satisfaction, he told the Nord, "We're moving."

"In what direction?"

And the Deacon shrugged grandly. "I haven't the foggiest idea."

"Then why . . . ?"

"Get serious!" the Deacon said. "I'm not telling those animals we haven't figured out the map yet. But I gotta keep 'em busy, till I do."

Down on the deck, only one Smoker, in goggles and jacket, remained. He stood just below them, staring up. It was as if he was not aware the speech was over.

"Who *is* that?" the Deacon demanded of the Nord. Then he yelled down. "Why aren't you rowing?"

The Smoker took off his goggles, and the Nord gasped, "It's *him!*"

And it was, indeed, the Mariner.

Enola stepped forward, beaming. "Boy, are you guys in a lot of trouble!"

She rushed to the railing and began to wave hello enthusiastically. The Nord grabbed her, pulling her back.

"The gentleman guppy," the Deacon said.

"All I want is the girl," the Mariner said. "Copy the

101

map off her back first—I don't care! Just set us adrift and we'll call it even."

The Deacon leaned over the railing and practically screamed, "And what on this screwed-up Waterworld of ours makes you think I'm gonna give her to you?"

The Mariner pulled a flare from the Smoker jacket, and popped it alight. He held the glowing stick in front of him—and right over the refueling shaft.

"You know where this leads," the Mariner said, holding the spark-fizzing flare right over the opening. "I drop it, and . . . ka-boom."

The Deacon merely smiled down. "Let's not do anything . . . rash, here. I mean, are you sure she's worth all this trouble?"

"Better listen to him," Enola said. "If he says he'll do it, he'll do it."

"I mean, do you *really* want this kid?" the Deacon asked him, reasonably enough. "After all, she never shuts up!"

"I've noticed," the Mariner granted.

"So what is it, the map? You had her long enough to copy it a hundred times!"

"She's my friend."

The Nord was clutching the railing, glaring down at the man who held out the glowing flare over the hole. "He's bluffing—"

"He's not bluffing," the child's voice chimed. "He *never* bluffs."

"Shut up!" the Deacon said. "I don't think you're gonna drop that torch down that hole, fish-man."

"And why is that?"

"Because you may be stupid," the Deacon said, "but you're not crazy."

"You should've smiled when you said that," the Mariner said.

And he dropped the flare into the shaft.

10

The Deacon's cry—"*Noooooooo!*"—sent his Smoker advisors scrambling through a doorway off the bridge. But the Nord and a pair of the Deacon's most trusted guards remained at their leader's side.

"Don't just stand there!" the Deacon shouted. "*Get him!*"

Down on the deck, the Mariner had taken off running. The Nord and the two Smoker guards stormed down the bridge steps after him.

Meanwhile, the glowing fiery flare tumbled down the refueling shaft, rickety-rattling down its long, deep path. Finally it splashed into the Deacon's lake of oil.

A storm of flame exploded, igniting a larger explosion that sent a fireball shattering through a bulkhead. Roaring explosions began deep in the ship, and began working their way up, as fire and destruction shook the *'Deez.*

The Mariner had seen the Nord and the pair of Smokers coming down the metal stairs after him. He ducked down a hatchway that had been sawed in the deck. Then he ran down a corridor onto a catwalk.

He needed to stay just below deck. His goal was to get back up there, up onto the bridge. He wasn't sure what had happened to Enola, and he had to find her.

Smoke was seeping up through rust-holes in the floor. He rounded a corner, stopping short at a gaping hole that suddenly ended the corridor.

Reluctantly, he backtracked. He took stairs down to a walkway that took him deeper into the recesses of the dying ship than he cared to hazard.

A patrol of Smokers came rushing down the walkway toward him, firing handguns. Bullets pinged around him. The Mariner returned fire, noticing a dangling pulley chain nearby.

He leapt for one strand of it and clung to it. The pulley carried him down, as shots whizzed by his head. Then a shotgun blasted a chain link apart.

His lifeline went limp and started twirling downward as he leapt to the other strand of pulley chain. The chain took him down, but he knew the ride was temporary. Before long the snapped strand would work through the pulley wheel, and drop him to his death.

There was a walkway two floors below. He swung on the chain, trying to maneuver himself over that walkway. He could drop there, with relative safety . . .

But just then the bright yellow eyes of a rumbling beast came bearing down upon him.

It was a car! A big, patched-together automobile! The Mariner had seen cars before, but dead ones: rusty, seaweed-draped relics in the dead cities he explored.

This car was very much alive, its engine thundering. The Nord was at the wheel, grinning behind the curved glass windscreen.

And the Mariner was unintentionally swinging directly into its path.

Then the pulley chain ran out, and swung the Mariner up and over the nose of the massive car. The beast missed him by inches! The now-slack chain deposited the Mariner in a pile on the metal floor.

The car spun around, to make another pass at him.

Its metal wheels threw brilliant sparks as the great machine came bearing down ominously on him. The Mariner got to his feet now, raised his pistol and fired. The bullet pierced the glass windscreen. The Nord struggled to see through the spiderwebbed windscreen, the car weaving and careening.

The Mariner rolled out of its path as the vehicle crashed into a metal beam.

The Mariner took off running.

He scrambled up a stairway. He began working his

way through the maze of corridors, trying to find his way back to the bridge.

The ship was starting to shake, to tip. The few Smokers he encountered offered him no resistance. They were too busy running.

Then he saw them! Fifty yards away, on an open stairway, the Deacon was dragging Enola up. The Mariner didn't call out. Neither the Deacon nor the child had spotted him. He still had surprise on his side . . .

The Deacon dragged Enola back out onto the bridge of the ship.

"See that?" he said, pointing to a plane on the deck. "That's your salvation."

And he hauled her down the steps, from the bridge onto the deck.

Moments later, the Mariner bolted onto the bridge. He leaned against the harpoon gun mounted there. His eyes slowly scanned the disorder on the deck below, as Smokers tried to find their way to safety or escape. Many were just leaping overboard.

Then he spotted the Deacon, at the seaplane. The Smoker leader was positioning Enola in the rear of the plane, in the gunner's seat.

The seaplane might as well have been a million miles away, at the other end of the deck! How could the Mariner get there in time?

Then he blinked. He was leaning against the answer!

What he needed was gathered for him in a supply box beside the harpoon gun. He grabbed a harpoon shaft, tied heavy line to the end of it, and loaded up the big weapon.

Down on the deck, the Deacon was in the cockpit of the seaplane, wheeling it around for takeoff.

The Mariner loaded up the harpoon and fired. Line trailing after it, the harpoon thwacked into the deck. The plane was making its way down the runway, just beginning to pick up speed. But the harpoon and its line stretched way out ahead of the plane.

The Mariner tied the harpoon line tight on the rail of the bridge. From the open supply box, he took an iron bar, and climbed over the rail. He slipped the iron bar over the line, and held onto either side of the bar.

And he jumped.

Sliding down the stretched line, the Mariner streaked over the deck. He was doing his best to outrace the seaplane.

The Deacon, at the controls, was cursing at the sight of the Mariner. The seaplane was headed for the curved launch ramp, building speed. . . .

The Mariner let go and landed nimbly to the deck. He quickly gathered up a pile of cable he'd spotted from the bridge. Working fast, the Mariner looped the cable's end around a post. He yanked it taut, so that it stretched out like a leg hoping to trip up an unwary walker.

The plane's landing gear slammed into the cable! Both wheels were sheared off with a metallic screech. The seaplane skidded on its belly up the launching ramp, where it teetered.

Then it fell! It landed on its side, off the end of the ramp, crashing into the bow. A wing snapped, and the engine was crushed—the plane was permanently grounded.

The go-juice in that plane could turn it into a fireball in moments. The Mariner had to get the child out of there!

The Deacon was slumped, unconscious, at the wheel. The child was frightened but unhurt. The Mariner pulled her out of the wreckage.

"Can you walk?" he asked her.

"I can *run!*" she said, smiling.

But he knew there was nothing to smile about. The ship was coming apart around them. The deck was heaving, explosions below deck rocking the ship. Then they heard an awful voice.

"If I can't have Dryland," the Deacon said, "you think I'm gonna let some walking catfish have it?"

The Smoker commander had a flare gun in one hand, pointed right at them. Burnt, his clothes in tatters, the Deacon rose from the rubble of the plane.

Then an oil-filled bottle, stuffed with a fiery rag, came hurtling from the sky like a hailstone! It slammed into the deck almost at the Deacon's feet, and exploded, throwing the Deacon sprawling backward.

Astounded and relieved, the Mariner and the child looked up at the sky.

There, sailing above the deck of the *'Deez*, was Old Gregor's balloon!

But this was a new, bigger, battle-ready basket with metal protecting both the basket and the underside of the balloon itself. Over the bullet-proof armor peeked Gregor, Helen, and the atoll Enforcer.

"Enola!" Helen called, dropping a line over the side.

Before they could grab hold, a massive blast erupted. A flower of fire bloomed up midway through the deck, cutting the ship in two.

Suddenly, the half of the deck the Mariner, Enola, and the Deacon found themselves on turned into a gigantic slide. All three went slipping, tumbling down toward the edge of the torn-apart deck.

The Mariner grabbed the dangling line. "Enola!"

Enola latched onto his waist.

And the Deacon completed the chain, grabbing onto Enola's leg.

"You'll never escape from me!" the Deacon yelled at her.

"You talk too much," she shouted, and kicked at him.

The Deacon went sliding down the deck and

dropped off the edge. It took a long time before he splashed.

With Enola clutching his waist, the Mariner climbed the dangling rope, leaving the deck behind. Bullets whizzed around them, aimed at the armored balloon they were heading for.

But the Mariner, with Helen's help, half climbed, half got pulled, into the basket. And he brought Enola along with him. Bullets were pinging against the metal plating.

"Don't worry," Gregor said. "We can't be harmed."

That was when a bullet severed a line. The basket tipped suddenly, throwing Enola off balance.

"Noooo!" Helen cried, reaching out for the girl. The Mariner reached for Enola, too. But it was too late.

Enola had spilled over the side, and she plummeted helplessly. She plopped into the water, and the sound was less a splash than a gulp, as if the sea had swallowed her.

Meanwhile, the Deacon had survived his slide into the ocean. And he had found a bobbing, abandoned jetski to ride. He was watching, waiting to see if the child would surface.

Then she did, sputtering, flailing at the water.

The Deacon gunned his engine, even as he waved other Smokers on jetskis to join him. From four directions, a trio of Smokers and their leader closed in on the tiny, water-treading target.

112

Above, the mariner was reeling in the bullet-snapped line. It wasn't rope, but something very precious in Waterworld: Rubber. He tied the end of the line around his ankles.

"What are you—" the Enforcer began.

But Helen knew. She smiled tightly, and nodded her support. He nodded back, and in as graceful a swan dive as Waterworld had ever seen, he plunged from the basket into the sky. The rubber line trailed after him like an eel in close pursuit.

Enola, treading water skillfully, was staring in fear at the jetskis closing in on her, howling closer.

The Mariner yelled, "Enola!"

And she glanced up as he dipped down and caught her by the arms. Then the rubber line recoiled, snapping the Mariner and his precious catch back into the sky.

Right before he collided with the other three jetskis, the Deacon raised his arms in protest.

Then he was lost in the orange and red and blue fireball that cannoned into the sky, narrowly missing the hovering balloon.

The Enforcer and Helen hauled the Mariner and Enola in over the side of the basket. Helen wrapped the child in her arms and held her very close.

Enola looked back at the Mariner. "I was swimming!"

He nodded, smiling. "I noticed."

113

Then they watched as, below, the stern of the broken ship gurgled beneath the surface. Soon nothing was left of the Deacon's once-grand empire except floating debris.

And before long, bright stars led their way. The balloon sailed, but not toward New Oasis. Everyone was asleep but the Mariner.

He was steering.

He had set a course, based upon a certain map. . . .

11

Several days later, as the balloon emerged from the clouds, a tropical mirage appeared before them.

Only it was not a mirage.

It was an island . . . *not an atoll*, but land—dry land.

Dryland.

The island was mostly a mountain, a mist-hazed mountain that glimmered with green. And there was a glowing white-sand beach with trees lining it.

Soon they had landed, and were witnessing it all, firsthand.

Water cascaded over rocks into a pool. It was magnificent! But somehow the Mariner's feet felt unsure on this . . . this . . . *earth*.

Old Gregor knelt at the pool, scooping up water in his cupped hands. "Fresh! All of this—*fresh!*"

The Enforcer called out, "I've found something!"

And with Helen in the lead, Enola trailing after, they moved up the hillside.

Gregor looked back at the Mariner. "Have you noticed?" the old man asked, gesturing to the ground. "It doesn't move!"

"I've noticed," the Mariner said.

They moved into a clearing. Suddenly a thundering shook the earth! The Mariner, startled, leaned on a tree to keep his balance. A herd of four-legged beasts, with wild eyes and flowing manes and rippling muscles, galloped by!

"Horses!" Helen shouted, joyfully. "And look there!"

Off to one side was a gathering of yellow-brown dwellings.

"Huts," Helen identified them. "This is what was known as a 'village.'"

But it was Gregor and the Enforcer who first entered one of the huts.

The Mariner had no interest. Something else had caught his eye, something half hidden in the weeds.

A boat. Barely more than a canoe, but with outrigger fittings.

Helen, with Enola at her side, entered the thatched hut, curious to see what Old Gregor and the Enforcer had found.

A pair of skeletons guarded a table littered with objects. One object caught Helen's attention—a paper with a map on it, identical to the markings on Enola's back.

116

"They . . . they must have known they were dying," Gregor said, his tone respectful.

"We should put them under the ground," the Enforcer said. "I have heard that that was their way, the land people."

"It was," Helen affirmed.

Enola did not cry. She merely walked to the table and popped open a small carved-wood box.

When the lid opened, something within the box played a lovely tune.

It was Enola's song, the song she sang to the wind.

"I'm home," the child said, quietly.

Helen looked at Gregor. His eyes, like her eyes, were brimming with tears. He nodded to Helen, as if to say, *We're all home.*

Then Helen frowned; someone was missing.

She found the Mariner on the beach. He was pushing a small boat, across the sand, toward the blue of the sea.

"I don't understand," she said.

Mildly surprised, he turned and gazed at her. "What don't you understand?"

"You brought us here. You belong here as much as any of us." She shrugged. "Maybe more."

He started pushing the little boat across the sand, again.

She followed, but didn't help him. "What are you

looking for? What do you think you can find out there?"

He looked out at the glistening water. "Gregor once said that there might be others like me, somewhere."

"Oh . . ."

He bestowed a smile on her. "If I run across others like you—others with hope, and courage—I'll tell them about this place. And how one woman found it."

She held back the tears. "We found it together."

He nodded. "Yes we did."

Soon, Helen, Gregor, and the Enforcer were parading onto the beach with supplies they'd gathered for the Mariner. But Enola was not helping. She was sitting on a log, staring out to sea.

The Mariner went to her and said, "For the first time in your life, you have nothing to say?"

She said nothing.

"Sing that song of yours," he said.

"You hate that song."

"I like it when you sing it."

He knelt down beside her, closer.

"Enola . . ." He touched her arm. ". . . I have to go now."

Now she looked at him. Her big blue eyes were clouded with tears. "But . . . you came back for me!"

"Of course I did," he said. "You're my friend."

And she threw herself into his arms, and the tears flowed.

"Why . . . why are you leaving us?"

He patted her back. "Because I don't belong here."

The child's lower lip trembled. "I . . . I can't change your mind, can I?"

"No."

She stood and showed him something she'd tucked behind her back.

The music box.

She popped open the lid and the box played her tune.

"Take this gift," she said. "And think of me."

Then she kissed him, and ran away, still in tears.

The Mariner made his way to the little boat, where Helen was waiting. Gregor and the Enforcer walked up. The old inventor was lugging a sack over his shoulder.

"I have something for you, too."

The old man plopped the sack heavily on the sand.

"It's dirt," Gregor said. "Don't trade it all in one place. Or maybe you should. That way you'll have a reason to come back and visit us."

The Enforcer stepped forward and extended his hand awkwardly. "It's all I have to offer, drifter."

"It's enough," the Mariner said, and the two warriors shook hands.

Gregor and the Enforcer took their leave.

The Mariner continued packing the supplies his friends had so generously gathered while Helen stood, watching.

"I . . . I have something for you, too. Something you may need on your journey."

"I'd feel better," he said, "if I had something to offer as trade . . ."

"No. This is free."

"There's nothing free in—"

She said. "Let this be a first."

His eyes locked on hers.

"It's a name," she said.

From the mountaintop they watched him, Helen and Enola. Hand in hand, they watched as his boat made its way across the shimmer of blue, into the mist.

Even after he'd disappeared, the woman and child stood, watching, holding hands.

"That name," Enola said. "Where'd you get it from?"

"An old, old story, about a great warrior who returned from battle."

"An old story?"

"Yes."

"Tell me, Helen. Tell me the story."

And Helen did. When she had finished, Helen took Enola's hand, and they moved into the trees, and down toward the village. As they went, Enola sang, but her song had changed.

"There is a boy," she sang, "lives in the wind, in the wind . . ."

EPILOGUE

. . . There is a boy, lives in the wind, his mother is the moon.

What is that, my children? What was the story Helen told the girl?

Well, a great warrior had just set sail when the water god cursed him. For ten years the warrior drifted on the seas, unable to find his way home.

Yes, it is a sad story . . . but it has a happy ending.

At last, the gods took pity on him. They called up a warm wind that blew him home—to his family. And you know what? He never left them, or his home, again.

His name?

Ulysses.

Yes, that *was the name Helen gave the Mariner.*

Did he ever return?

Oh, but my children—old Enola tires of all this talk, and that's another *story. . . .*